# DANCES WITH DEMONS

## THE PHOENIX CHRONICLES

### LORI HANDELAND

# CHAPTER 1

$\mathcal{I}$ cried when they took away my children. Who wouldn't?

"Mom." Anna, my oldest, might be only nine, but she can roll her eyes like any sixteen-year-old. "We go to Mam and Pop's every summer for two weeks, and every summer you act like it's forever."

"It always feels like forever." I rubbed the sting of tears from my eyes. I couldn't help it. Anna and her brothers were all I had left of Max. But, to be fair, they were all Max's parents had left of him either. So, for the final two weeks of each summer, I allowed my in-laws to drive away from Milwaukee with my babies.

Anna rolled her eyes again, but she allowed me to hug her, even kiss her forehead before squirming away and out the door in the wake of her grandfather.

The boys, Aaron and Benjamin—who'd recently decided he liked to be called Benji—were six and five, and they still allowed me to smooch on them for longer than Anna did. They always had. I ruffled their dark heads, so like Max's, and sent them on their way, then turned to face my mother-in-law, a woman who did not look in any way like she answered to the sweet granny name of *Mam*. If I hadn't wanted to keep on her good side, I would have been tempted to address her as *Cruella*. Not that she'd skinned any puppies lately, though I wouldn't put it past her.

Susan Murphy was tall, slim, and always perfectly put together, in control of herself and of anyone else she could manage. I doubted the woman ever left her house in anything less than full makeup and hair that she'd sprayed into an immovable coif. In comparison, I always appeared shorter, dumpier, and less put together than I actually was. I think she liked it that way. She'd certainly never liked me.

I'd hoped that once Max and I had children, Susan and I would bond. Hadn't happened. With my own parents living in Phoenix now, Max's were the closest relatives I had. You'd think we'd spend more time together.

But now that Max was dead, and I had opened a tavern/restaurant then had the bad taste to call it *Murphy's*—thus tarnishing their name—I doubted we'd ever be BFFs. I didn't mind so much. I had a BFF; I didn't need another. However, it would be nice if Susan would at least pretend not to loathe me.

"Megan." She lowered her head, a dismissal, a good-bye.

"If you have any problems," I said, following her to the door, then onto the porch and down the walk toward the waiting Lincoln Navigator, "just give me a call and I'll drive down."

"I doubt anything will come up that I can't manage."

The only thing Susan Murphy had ever been unable to manage was her only son. She hadn't wanted him to become a cop. If he just *had* to help people, why not become a lawyer? Because *they* were so helpful.

She'd gotten past Max's choice of profession, only to have him turn around and marry me.

In her defense, she'd been right about the occupation. Max had died in the line of duty. But the only thing he'd ever wanted more than that badge was me.

My eyes pricked again. God, I missed him. Some days were harder than others, and today was one of them.

"Who is that?" My mother-in-law's already chilly voice went ice age.

Quinn Fitzpatrick leaned against the side of my house. Tall, lean and dark, with eerily light green eyes that seemed to shine yellow in a certain light, he resembled a panther on the prowl. Until he moved. Then he usually tripped over his puppy feet, dropped a glass, knocked over a tray or worse. I'd never seen a more beautiful man with less grace in my life.

"New bartender."

I lifted my hand in hello. Quinn lifted his in return and smacked the gutter so hard it came apart. He caught the loose piece, cracked it against the house, then frowned at the dent. I sighed. He'd fix the thing so it would be better than before. Sometimes I thought he broke things on purpose just so he could improve them.

"He's very . . ." Susan's lips pursed. She glanced at me in suspicion. "Tell me you aren't sleeping with him."

I blinked. "Sleep . . . I . . . No!"

She rolled her eyes, and I saw where Anna had gotten it from. "The man is sex on parade."

"If he were in a parade he'd trip, fall into the tuba section, cause them to knock over the drums, and the entire band would end up in the lake."

"You expect me to believe that a man who looks like that does nothing more than pour drinks?"

"He makes sandwiches too."

"Hi, Quinn!" Benji shouted.

Quinn waved and dropped the gutter on his foot.

"Bye, Quinn!" Aaron hung out the window.

"We'll see you in two weeks." Anna's smile was genuine. Even she had a soft spot for Quinn.

"It's right here I'll be when you come back." The slight Irish lilt that sometimes crept into his voice always made me want to close my eyes and beg him to keep talking. And not touch anything.

"He's Irish!" Susan accused.

"Quinn. Fitzpatrick." I spread my hands.

"You're Megan Murphy and you don't have an accent."

"But I do like potatoes."

"The children obviously know him well."

"He works everyday. He helps fix things around here." Usually after he broke them, but I kept that to myself. "They know him. They like him. He's . . . likeable."

"Do you like him?"

I glanced at Quinn as he laid the gutter on the ground and strode toward the garage where he kept his tools. He caught the toe of his large athletic shoes on a blade of grass and nearly kissed dirt. "I guess."

I'd never really thought of Quinn as anything other than a slightly klutzy first-shift bartender. Certainly, he was lovely to look at, even lovelier to listen to. But since Max had died I'd first been focused on getting through each day without dissolving into a puddle of agony. Once that was accomplished, my next job had been raising the children, then paying the bills.

I'd met Max while I was a waitress in a cop bar on the south side. We'd married, had children, lived, loved, laughed. Then he'd died. All I knew was being a wife, a mother, and running a bar. So I'd opened Murphy's.

It hadn't been easy. The hours were long and, to begin with, most of them were mine. I received a lot of law enforcement business since Max's former co-workers made Murphy's their new hangout, and his former partner, Liz Phoenix, had left the force—Max's death had been as hard on her as it had been on me—and taken a job as my dayshift bartender.

Liz blamed herself for Max's death though I never had. We'd become best friends; we always would be, even though she was now the leader of a group of demon killers pledged to save mankind from the Apocalypse. As I'd attended Catholic school, the approach of doomsday was less of a surprise to me than it had been to her.

My mother-in-law's sigh brought me back to my front yard. "I suppose it's time."

"Yes." I started walking toward the SUV. "I know you want to get on the road." I paused when I realized she hadn't moved and glanced back.

"I meant that it's time you moved on." Though the words were gentle, her face was . . . devastated.

"I don't—"

"Max is gone. He isn't coming back. You're alive, so are the children."

"Okay." I had no idea what she was trying to tell me beyond the obvious. Life went on.

Even when you didn't want it to.

* * *

QUINN FITZPATRICK STOOD JUST out of sight as he waited for Megan's in-laws to drive away with her children.

He'd felt her pain even before he'd turned the corner and seen the remnants of the tears in her eyes. He'd wanted to take her in his arms and make her every sadness fade away. But he knew better.

Even if she could look past the ghost of her precious Max and see Quinn, she would see the man he presented to the world. A loner with no past, an uncertain future. A man who worked for cash. Not that he needed cash, which was why he slipped it back into the till whenever Megan was gone, however it would cause even more suspicion to work for free. He had no home, no friends, no family. Because he wasn't yet truly a man.

He had been sent to protect Megan Murphy, nothing more.

That he had fallen in love with her was both a blessing and his curse. His mistress—

"Liz," he corrected. She hated it when he called her by that title, but he was ancient and such an address was her right. Nevertheless, she had told him not to kneel, not to bow, never to call her *mistress* again. It marked her as special in a world where special would get you killed.

Liz Phoenix was the leader of the light. She helmed a group of seers and demon killers known as the federation, tasked with saving humanity from the evil beings that wished to bring about the end of this world. Because Liz loved Megan, those beings would either try to use Megan against Liz, or, perhaps, just kill her. Quinn would never, ever, let that happen.

"Fitzpatrick?"

Quinn blinked. How long had he been standing with the hammer in his hand, daydreaming? Long enough for the in-laws to drive away and Megan to call for him.

He strode around the corner and slammed into her so hard she flew backward, landing on her ample—and luscious—backside. Quinn cursed in Gaelic, then reached out to help her with the hand that held the hammer.

Had he tried to seem clumsy so many times that he'd actually become so? Apparently.

"Spit out the gum." Megan clambered to her feet on her own, dusting off that backside he spent far too much time lusting after.

Quinn's lips curved at her usual quip. She often teased that he was unable to walk and chew gum at the same time. He did his best to appear so.

"I'm going to start the stew while you repair your latest . . ." She waved a hand at the piece of dented gutter that lay on the ground.

"Aye," he agreed.

As it was Sunday, they opened at four instead of eleven, not only because it was the Sabbath but because Megan made Irish stew. Quinn had not tasted the likes of a stew such as hers since he'd last been in Ireland. He tried to remember when that had been and couldn't. When time was eternal the days, weeks, months, years, decades and so on all blended together.

Megan made the traditional stew with mutton, which meant the brew had to simmer atop the stove for a good portion of the day. But ah, when it was finished, 'twas well worth the wait. Folks would come from all over southeastern Wisconsin to sample Megan's stew of a Sunday eve. When combined with a pint drawn just right, there was nothing better on a cold winter or a warm summer night.

Quinn took his time fixing the gutter. He had long been a creature of the night, had only recently been able to walk beneath both the sun and the moon. But he so enjoyed the sunlight. Especially when it burnished Megan's red hair to a shade resembling maple leaves in late October. Her eyes were a midnight sky and—

He slammed the hammer into his thumb and cursed. "*Ciach ort!*"

What was wrong with him? He had never in all of his years on the earth ever been so enamored of a woman. Why her? Why here? Why now?

Because Megan was not only beautiful but brave. Her husband gunned down in the street, she'd been left alone with three young children. Certainly there were mornings when fear lived in her eyes. There were nights he stood outside, watching her pace beyond the windows of her home until dawn threatened, but she managed. Megan always managed.

He had come to adore her children nearly as much as he adored her. Perhaps because he had never had any of his own and probably never would.

Quinn finished his task, returned the tools to the shed and strolled toward Murphy's. The tavern was only a block from the house. Convenient for all concerned.

As he opened the door, he wondered why he didn't smell

onions frying, then he heard a faint sound, like the hitch of breath, a smothered cry. Ach, hell. Megan was enjoying a solitary sob over being parted from her bairns, and he'd nearly blundered into it. As a woman such as she would not welcome the intrusion, he hovered just inside the door, trying not to listen, not to think of the tears rolling down her cheeks. How would they taste?

He licked his lips, rubbed his neck, and fought the response of his body—both man and beast. Then that bit of beast that remained, despite all his attempts to overcome it, caught a scent that disturbed him. Sharp and wild, like nothing he had ever smelled before. It wasn't right that it should be here.

Quinn moved forward on silent, sure feet, ears pricked. Those cries he'd heard continued. They were distressed, to be sure, and when he reached the kitchen, he saw why.

The man with his hand over Megan's mouth appeared to be just a man, but he was more. Quinn felt it in the quiver that came over him at the very tip of every hair on his body—head to toe. Quinn was a DK, a demon killer, had been from the day he took this form. Within the federation, those such as he worked with a seer, a being of powerful psychic power who could identify the demon beneath the skin of man and woman.

Demons had been around for a long, long time. In days of old —the Old Testament that is—God sent the Grigori, angels known as watchers, to earth to keep an eye on the humans. They lusted after them instead and were banished by God to Tartarus—the lowest, locked level of hell. But they left a bit of themselves behind.

The offspring of those fallen angels and humans are called Nephilim, and they're still here; they are what the federation fights. All those legends about vampires and werewolves and other seemingly fantastical, supernatural creatures are true. The Nephilim might look like other men and women on the street, but they aren't.

The war for humanity had begun. The clock ticking down to

doomsday had started. The Apocalypse was nigh. The federation was trying to stop it just as hard as the Nephilim were trying to cause it. At the moment, the bad guys were winning.

There had been a recent purge. Quinn's seer was dead, which was one of the reasons he had been sent here. He knew a demon when he felt one.

The majority died by a few tried and true methods—silver, decapitation, dismemberment. If one didn't work, Quinn was always perfectly happy to try another.

He retrieved the long, slim, lethal, silver knife he kept hidden behind the bar beneath the hat he wore sometimes when he hadn't had time to cut his hair. Then he crept out the front door and around to the back. He saw no others lurking about, but that didn't mean there weren't. However his concern now was Megan. He should never have left her alone.

However, if he stuck too close to Megan, she shooed him away. He couldn't blame her. He'd done his best to appear less than he was, which had only succeeded in making him so much more than annoying.

Quinn snuck in the back, wondering why the fool had not just killed Megan and moved on, then he heard the thing speak.

"Where is the leader of the light?" The creature lifted his hand from Megan's mouth.

"Fuck you."

Why hadn't Megan screamed in an attempt to bring Quinn running? Because she thought he was incapable.

Quinn stepped inside, pressed the point of the knife to the man's neck. "Let her go."

Megan cursed. "Quinn, I'm—

The half-demon released her. It had no doubt smelled the silver.

"Free," Quinn finished. "Go."

She spun, frowning at the knife. "Where did you—?"

"Go," he ordered, and her frown deepened. "Call the authorities."

It would give her something to do. By the time anyone arrived, this beast would be ashes on the wind. If it couldn't be killed by silver the thing never would have released her.

Megan went into the bar. As soon as the door closed behind her Quinn murmured, "Are there more of you?"

The creature didn't answer. Quinn hadn't thought it would, but he had to try. He plunged the knife into the Nephilim's neck and it imploded, covering Quinn in gray grime. How he would explain that, Quinn wasn't sure, but anything that threatened Megan must die.

The being had to be some type of shifter—Lord alone knew what—as it had died by silver. He thought it odd that the beast had been asking about Liz. Usually his mistress left a trail of ashes behind her that was very hard to miss.

Quinn retrieved a dustpan and broom as he listened to Megan speak with emergency services. By the time they arrived even the ashes would be gone.

He stepped to the back door, pan full of Nephilim dust, to have his attention captured by a movement in the alley. The hair on his arms lifted again as the fellow smirked. Quinn didn't like that at all. He dropped the dustpan, ignoring the puff of ash across his shoes as he spun toward the kitchen. He sniffed, caught a hint of something wrong, then he heard the tick-tock.

Drawing on his preternatural speed, he sprinted into the bar, snatching Megan around the waist and lifting her easily from the ground.

"Quinn, I'm still—"

He leaped through the front door and raced across the street as Murphy's tavern blew upward, then rained in several thousand pieces from the sky.

# CHAPTER 2

*J* still held the phone in my hand when I landed in a yard across the street. I was so dazed I even lifted the thing to my ear. "Hello?"

No one answered. How could they when the base of the phone was still in Murphy's and most of Murphy's continued to rain in pieces all around us?

Quinn, who'd done some fancy twisting in the air, managing to land beneath me and not on top of me, cushioning my fall, removed the phone from my hand. He stared at it a moment as if he couldn't figure out what it was, then tossed it over his shoulder.

"Are you all right?" he asked.

"I—" I began and then stopped, unsure what to say. I was fine, but my tavern was toast. Which meant I wasn't fine at all.

"Megan?" He leaned in close, peering into my eyes with his eerie yellow gaze. As no one had yellow eyes, I understood that the shade was merely a reflection of the flames rising from the rubble.

Sirens wailed. They seemed very far away.

Quinn's long, gentle fingers ran over my head. His touch felt so good, I leaned into him. "Is there somewhere you hurt, *a ghrá?*"

I lifted my hand to my chest and rubbed at the ache there. He snatched my fingers, peered at them, then my chest. "Did a chunk of wood strike ye?"

His voice sounded more Irish by the minute. I liked it.

"Megan!" I lifted my gaze. His had gone chartreuse. "I see no blood."

"No," I agreed. "No blood."

I'd sweated every last drop I could spare into Murphy's.

The police arrived, then the fire department, and an ambulance. Make that two.

"Stay," Quinn said.

He needn't have. I couldn't have moved if I wanted to.

He sent the EMTs in my direction. While they checked me over I kept my gaze on the shell that was Murphy's and tried to think what to do.

"I got nothin'," I muttered.

The EMTs exchanged glances. One of them stayed with me, the other crossed to Quinn, said something. Quinn's eyes met mine and he strode toward me.

"You should lie down."

"All right." I stood then started toward the house. It wasn't until Quinn slid an arm about my waist and tugged me close that I realized I'd been zigzagging down the walk like a drunk. I'd seen enough zigzagging, and enough drunks, to know.

We reached my home. Quinn tried to lead me inside but I didn't want to go.

"Meggie," he murmured. He'd never called me that before. I liked it, along with the warm brush of his breath against my temple.

"I need air."

He didn't bother to ask where I would get it, just led me to the backyard and set me on the bench in the middle of the garden.

I'd dreamed of growing vegetables, never had managed it. At first I was lucky if I got in a shower each day, then I had my hands full with kids and Murphy's. Looked like I'd have plenty of time now.

The burble of laughter that escaped sounded more like a sob.

Quinn, who'd taken a step toward a police officer who'd followed us, stepped right back. I lifted a hand. "I'm okay."

I wasn't but I'd had plenty of experience with that lie. I'd become good at it. Apparently not good enough for Quinn. He stayed where he was.

I contemplated the overgrown garden. Something was missing. What? There'd never been anything here but weeds, lost baseballs and—

"My statue," I blurted, and Quinn stiffened.

I'd always assumed the black panther made of stone had come with the house. I certainly hadn't bought it. The thing was kind of odd, the shoulders sloped and somehow humanoid. However, when I sat in the garden the beast, tail curved around its sleek body, had kept me company. There'd been something about that statue, even with the eerie yellow-green shade of its eyes, that had soothed me.

"Someone stole my statue."

"Why would anyone want to take that ugly old thing?" Quinn asked.

"I liked it."

"Did ye now?" he murmured, and his palm ran over my hair.

"Sir?" The cop was so young I didn't know him. Max had been gone long enough that all the street cops were new.

Tears pricked my eyes, and I leaned into Quinn. I was so damn tired.

"I need to get your statement," the officer continued.

"Will ye be all right, Meggie?"

"I'm always all right."

"I'll be just here." Quinn pointed to where the young man

hovered at the edge of my property. "I'll not let you out of my sight again."

* * *

QUINN ANSWERED the policeman's questions, some of them even truthfully.

"The place went boom," Quinn said. "No idea why."

"How did you and Mrs. Murphy get out?"

"Ran."

"Why?"

"Intruder."

"Who is . . .?"

"Ashes."

The officer waited for more, and when he realized he wouldn't be getting it, thanked Quinn and went away.

"And the truth will set you free," Quinn murmured.

He kept his gaze on Megan as he withdrew his cell phone from his pocket and hit the first number on his favorites list. He didn't expect it to be answered, so when it was, and by the woman he'd called, he blinked for several seconds as Liz said, "Hello? Quinn? Hello?"

For an instant he thought the leader of the light was even more psychic than the rumors, then he remembered the annoying/useful invention known as caller ID.

"It is I, mis— Liz."

"Meg. Is she—?"

"Alive," he said. "There was a Nephilim, but he is dead."

"Isn't that why you're there? To kill the evil half demons? According to you, you've ended legion. Why call me about this one?"

Why indeed?

"When I came upon them he was demanding to know your whereabouts."

"Came upon?" she repeated, her voice deceptively quiet.

"Aye, but he will never touch anyone again."

"He touched her?" Quinn winced and didn't answer. "What else?"

Quinn told her everything as Megan stared at the garden. If he hadn't seen her shoulders rising and falling with each breath, he'd think she'd turned into the statue she seemed to mourn. He hadn't believed she'd even known it was there.

"Why are they searching for you, mistress?"

"They're always searching for me," Liz muttered. That she didn't correct his slip of the tongue in addressing her only proved how rattled she was by the turn of events. Probably as rattled as he.

"Why would they think Megan knows where you are?"

"They were fishing. I'm sure their next step was to-" He heard her swallow. He understood. The Nephilim's next step always involved human blood. "Take her and the children—"

"The children are with their grandparents for a fortnight."

"Excellent. By then I'll be . . ." Her voice trailed off. "Is there somewhere you can take her? Far away until I've figured this out?"

He thought "this" meant more than the Nephilim that had come here. There was something going on. With Liz, there always was.

"What's wrong?" he asked.

"We've got a situation."

"There's always a situation."

"Not like this."

He didn't care for what he heard in her voice—both despair and fear—something that should never be heard in the voice of a leader such as she. The circumstances must be dire. Though Quinn did not want to leave Megan, he had also foresworn himself to this cause during a time so ancient he only remembered it well in his dreams.

"Shall I come to you?"

Silence fell, and his fingers curled inward. He did not want to go, but he would if the leader of the light called. He must.

"I need you with Megan. Never leave her, Quinn. Never."

"Your wish is my command, mistress."

"Stop calling me that," she said, but there was a lack of heat to those words that frightened him.

He wished for more details. Who was dead this time? Why did her voice shake when he'd never heard it shake before? But he could also tell that she was in a hurry, had places to go, creatures to kill, and she would not waste time sharing anything with him now beyond orders.

"I'll send a DK to lurk at the senior Murphy's place," Liz continued.

"Send two."

"All right," she said slowly. "And you? Where will you be?"

"With Megan." Quinn hung up.

He knew exactly where to go, and the fewer people who knew about it the better.

In a normal world, Liz would never betray the woman she loved more than any other. But the world was no longer normal, and being the leader of the light meant Liz had pledged to sacrifice everyone, everything to save it. From what he'd heard in her voice, she'd already sacrificed so much she could hardly bear it. She could not survive another loss.

But then neither could he.

\* \* \*

NIGHT HAD FALLEN before the police and fire department were through with whatever it was they were doing. I suppose I could have figured it out if I'd wanted to, but a strange lethargy had come over me. I couldn't make myself care about anything.

Eventually, I'd allowed Quinn to lead me inside. I'd drunk the tea he'd made. I'd even talked to the children when he handed me a phone and ordered me to. I didn't say much beyond "uh-huh" after they told me of their adventures at the Lincoln Park Zoo and the Shedd Aquarium, then a murmured, "love you too" instead of good-bye. Saying good-bye right now gave me the wiggies.

I would not tell them about *Murphy's* yet. Why spoil their visit? There'd be time enough to discuss ruin when they returned.

"I've called the insurance folk." Quinn came into the kitchen with my overnight bag. It looked in damn good shape. It should. I hadn't used it since my wedding night. "I told them to contact me by phone if they have any more questions."

"All right," I agreed, still not getting the significance of the bag.

"The police as well."

Why didn't the police want to talk to me?

"Don't they need a description of the man in the kitchen?"

The one who'd asked me about Liz. He'd probably been a half-demon, maybe even a whole one.

I giggled then slapped my hand over my mouth, the movement reminding me of the instant when *he* had done it. Oddly, I hadn't been afraid until Quinn showed up.

I knew the score. Quinn didn't.

"That man is dead."

I remembered the long, silver blade in Quinn's hand. "Where did you get the knife?" It had not matched any of mine.

"Does it matter?"

I thought it did, but I wasn't sure why.

"You killed the man?" If he had I didn't think the police would have left yet.

"Ach, no. Me and the intruder were awaitin' the authorities." He turned his gaze to his ash covered shoes. "I smelled gas, then the fool lit a cigarette."

That explained why he'd come running out of the kitchen. It

did not explain how he'd snatched me up, then run so fast without tripping. I wasn't sure anything could.

He lifted his eyes to mine. "The man who would have stolen from you is dead."

Quinn believed the Nephilim had been a thief. Worked for me.

"No reason for you to think of him anymore at all," he continued.

Good. Because whenever I thought of him, my stomach felt a bit queasy. Nevertheless . . .

"I should call Liz."

His forehead creased. "Liz?"

"You met her at Anna's birthday party last month." Had it only been a month?

He continued to look confused. "She arrived with that teenaged boy. Luther?"

Who'd been a lion shifter, but we weren't going to get into that.

"And a baby," he said slowly.

She'd been something too. One minute an infant, the next a kitten. According to Liz, Faith could turn into any animal when touched by something that depicted it. I'd found this out when I'd nearly covered the kid with a blanket of dancing blue baby elephants. If Liz hadn't stopped me my house would have been in as many pieces as my bar.

I slapped my palm over my mouth before another sob escaped.

Quinn set a hand on my shoulder. "Maybe you should lie down before your flight."

I lowered my arm. "What flight?"

"I've booked you on one that leaves at half nine from O'Hare. By the time you arrive in Dublin it'll be nigh onto noon."

"Dublin, Ireland?"

"Is there another, love?"

"I think there's a Dublin, Ohio."

"And why would that be?"

"My thoughts exactly," I muttered.

"You should rest. I'll wake you before we head to the airport."

"Why am I going to Ireland?"

"Haven't you always wanted to?"

I had, but how did he know that?

"Don't say you can't, because you can. The children are gone; the bar is . . ." He paused.

"Gone too."

"Aye," he agreed. "But not for long, lass. Not forever. We will rebuild it."

"We?"

The idea of Quinn building—tripping, falling, dropping things—made me smile until I remembered that he hadn't tripped, fallen or dropped anything, including me, since this whole nightmare had started.

"Did you believe I'd leave you in a lurch?"

He wouldn't. I knew that as well as I knew my name was Megan Margaret O'Malley Murphy. Say that five times fast. I dare you. Even the priest had bungled it during my wedding.

Quinn led me from the kitchen and up the stairs. At the door to my room, he paused. "I have a few errands. I'll lock up tight, be back in plenty of time." He urged me inside, drawing the door shut behind me. His steps retreated; the door closed downstairs. By the time I reached the window, he was gone.

A glint in the garden drew my attention. The moon shone off curved, black stone.

The statue was back.

# CHAPTER 3

"*J*'m not going to Ireland without you," I said.

"There was only one seat left on the flight. I'll be along directly."

I wasn't certain why I was going to Ireland at all, except Quinn had been right. I'd always wanted to, and right now I didn't have anything else to do. If I stayed in Milwaukee, with no work, no Liz, no kids . . . It wouldn't be pretty.

During the hour-plus drive from Milwaukee to Chicago's O'Hare Airport, Quinn had explained that his family kept a cottage in the countryside not far from Dublin. I could fly in; he'd have a friend pick me up and take me there.

"I doubt your family will welcome strange company."

"You aren't that strange."

"Ha," I deadpanned. Showed what he knew. My best friend was a demon fighter.

There'd been a demon in my bar. And it wasn't the first time. I couldn't bring that down on Quinn's family. I hadn't wanted to bring it down on him.

"You needn't worry, lass." His fingers tightened on the

steering wheel. "My family is dead. There'll be no one there but you."

"And you, right?"

For as many times in the past nine years since I'd had my first child that I'd wished for a week, a day, an hour, hell a minute alone, the idea of it now scared me. And that it did ... scared me even more.

"Aye," he murmured.

He was determined to get me to Ireland. I'd argued that I didn't have the money for the flight. He said he'd used his frequent flyer miles. How he'd gathered them, I had no idea. During the time he'd been with me he'd never taken more than a day off a week, and then only because I made him. There was also the issue of my paying him cash, which had made me wonder if he was in some kind of trouble. But if it were terrible trouble, he wouldn't have frequent flyer miles, now would he? The instant he tried to get on a plane, TSA would have been all over him.

On the one hand, I didn't want to go without him. On the other hand, why was he going at all? He was my employee. I'd never seen him as anything but.

Until today when he'd saved my life.

Was gratitude behind my sudden desire to take his hand and not let go? Perhaps nerves or fear or even loneliness. My kids were away; my business was dust. Liz had not picked up when I called, nor returned my message. Considering her occupation, she could be dead and might never pick up or call back again.

I shuddered. What would I do without her? Same thing as the rest of the world.

Die.

"Are you afraid of flying, love?"

Quinn's accent was getting more Irish by the minute. And that wasn't the only thing that seemed different about him. Since Murphy's had gone boom, he hadn't tripped once. Which was just strange. Klutzy teens would grow into their too large feet and overly long limbs. But grown men, and women, did not become graceful overnight. How had he?

"Megan?"

"Hmm?"

He brushed back a curl and his fingertips traced my brow, causing the shudder to return, but for a far different reason. Certainly I'd noticed how beautiful he was the instant he'd stumbled into Murphy's. While I might be overworked and undersexed, I wasn't blind or stupid. However, a man such as Quinn would never be interested in a short, dumpy, redheaded mother of three. He wasn't blind or stupid either.

Nevertheless, the slide of his fingers, softer than they should be for a working man, the nearness of his long, lithe body, the scent of a man—tangy, a bit wild—made me remember that I hadn't had sex since Max died. I hadn't missed it either. Or had I?

I lifted my gaze, saw concern in his, and stepped back. I'd been swaying toward him, face lifted, eyes drifting closed as if waiting for our very first kiss. I wondered momentarily if I'd hit my head when Murphy's exploded. It would explain a few things.

Like the disappearing/reappearing panther statue that didn't even belong to me. Or my bizarre impression that Quinn had grown graceful. The equally bizarre sensation that he had touched me as a man touched a woman. Not only was he my employee, but he had to be at least five years my junior. He was being kind and perhaps a bit mercenary—if I lost my mind, or worse, there'd be no rebuilding of Murphy's and there went his job.

"Are you afraid to fly?" he repeated.

"I don't know." I moved back even more. "I've never flown."

His fingers hovered in the air in front of my face for a moment before he let his hand fall away. "Never?"

"Everything I've ever wanted was here." I frowned. "There?" I wasn't home anymore. Right now I felt like I might never be home again. Home was Murphy's, and it was gone.

Quinn let out a breath, shoved his hands into his pockets and lifted his gaze to the starry sky. "I understand."

Then he handed me my overnight bag, my boarding pass, my passport and walked away.

Too bad I didn't.

* * *

QUINN MET Ronan Doyle at the cargo shipping bay.

The federation had agents in place all over the world. Though they had lost many of their number in the recent purge, they had not lost Ronan. Quinn, who had known the fellow since his earliest days in Ireland, thought that perhaps it was because Ronan was too damned quarrelsome to die. Or maybe it was just that he was very hard to kill.

As time went on, the Nephilim had mated with humans, producing breeds. Breeds had mated with other humans and with one another. The added influx of humanity with each successive generation diluted the demon enough so that breeds could make a choice about which side they fought for. Many of them were DKs, like Ronan.

He was the product of two breeds, which meant that while he might have more human blood than most, he also had more inherited abilities. His mother had been a selkie—a seal shifter—and had bestowed his given name, Ronan meaning *little seal* in the Gaelic. However, there was very little that was little about Ronan —perhaps because his father had been a troll of Viking descent. Though his last name, Doyle, was common enough in the Emerald Isle, it had originally been Ó *Dubhghaill*, or son of the evil, dark foreigner.

Ronan stood six-four in bare feet, six-six in his heavy heeled motorcycle boots. He liked to dress in black because the grease blended in.

He had been orphaned young, taken in by a gremlin and

taught the trade. To most, a gremlin was a being that fouled up motors. In truth, they could only do so because they understood them.

Ronan had also learned ill humor from his gremlin foster father. The original title of gremlin being *gruaimín*, or ill-humored little fellow.

Despite Ronan's fearsome appearance and snarly nature, or perhaps because of it, Quinn trusted him as he did few others. Ronan had no time for nonsense. He did the job and went away. Which was why Quinn had called the man last eve.

"Everything set?" Quinn asked.

Ronan merely quirked a thick, inky eyebrow—everything about Ronan was dark except his eerily light hazel eyes—kicked the sturdy box on the ground with one booted foot, then lifted the packing tape gun dwarfed by his huge hand. On a normal man that hand would have been rough and scarred by the years he'd worked on engines of every type—cars, cycles, planes—not a one could hide their mysteries from Ronan Doyle. However, his hand was smooth and soft as a child's. Like Quinn, Ronan could heal most of his own wounds.

"The box will be collected in Dublin and delivered to the cottage as ordered." Ronan had once possessed an accent as Irish as the one that sometimes slipped into Quinn's voice, but he'd always been better able to keep it out, perhaps because his father had spoken Norse.

"Who will be collecting it?"

"Ben." Quinn winced, and Ronan's lips curved in the depths of his forever-black beard. Beneath it, Ronan was as handsome as the prince he'd once been. He was also forever young. Same as Quinn. "Who else could be trusted with such?"

Quinn lowered his head. He trusted Ronan's foster father nearly as much as he trusted Ronan. He just didn't like him. He had met many people in his life. He'd met an equal number of demons. Not one of them was as ill-humored as that gremlin.

"It's whispered that the leader of the light revealed the truth of our world to her dearest friend," Ronan continued.

"Whispered where?" Quinn cast Ronan a frown. "By whom?"

The whispers were true, but it would not do for everyone to know it. Most members of the federation were ancient and that was not how things were done. Secrets were secrets for a reason.

"Megan Murphy saw what she should not have, yet she was not sanctioned."

Sanctioned meant brainwashed, banished, or worse. A trickle of unease made Quinn shift his suddenly tense shoulders.

"It wasn't her fault," he said.

"Fault has nothing to do with it."

"I am her guardian." Quinn drew himself up. The tip of his head only reached Ronan's shoulder. "I have sworn nothing will hurt her while I am near."

"Then you'd best get near, hadn't you?"

# CHAPTER 4

*I* swore I'd just finished supper and closed my eyes when the lights inside the plane went on and the flight attendant announced breakfast.

"We will land in Dublin in an hour where the local time will be just after noon."

Quinn had not only had enough mileage for my ticket but also an upgrade to business class. I'd enjoyed the extra leg room, despite my lack of leg. I'd taken a short walk through the plane before the movie had begun, and those in coach were packed like fish in a barrel. Not that I'd ever seen any fish in a barrel, but I could imagine. Better now than ever before.

When I'd returned to my seat, I'd enjoyed several glasses of complimentary red wine, which might explain why supper and breakfast had seemed so close together. I'd snoozed my way across the Atlantic.

As I exited the plane the promised hour later, with no bag but the one on my shoulder, I reached the exit well ahead of the crowd. Only when I stepped into the hazy sunlight did I remember that I had no idea where I was going. A friend of Quinn's was supposed to meet me. I had no idea who that was, and it occurred to me now to wonder how this friend would recognize me.

Tiny redhead with blue eyes? I glanced around. There were about a million of us.

"Hell," I muttered. What if no one picked me up? I had no contact information—not a name or phone number—no money except American—and not much of it—and my only credit card was maxed out.

I returned to the airport terminal. Comfy chairs surrounded a coffee shop, bordered by a bar with less comfy chairs. I'd just camp out in one or both until Quinn came. I hoped that would be before I was required to purchase anything. Maybe there was a place to exchange dollars for whatever they used here.

"Mrs. Murphy?" I turned, along with half a dozen other women. Murphys in Ireland were apparently as plentiful as redheads. "*Megan* Murphy."

The others lost interest. Which was unfortunate, because one of them might have given me a hint as to the location of whoever was calling my name. I couldn't see him.

"Is there a Megan Murphy here?"

"Yes!" I lifted my hand as if in a classroom.

The crowd now bunched at the exit shifted. Shoving ensued, followed by a few Gaelic curses. I recognized them from the times Quinn had dropped things. Then a little man popped free. He resembled one of those troll dolls that had freaked me out as a child. Squishy face, large shiny dark eyes and red-blonde hair that stood straight up. At least it wasn't a migraine inducing shade of neon. Did he have a jewel in his belly button? One glance at his expression convinced me not to ask.

He strode over to stand directly in front of me, although strode wasn't the right word. Strode was for long-legged, large fellows. The top of this man's head barely reached my collarbone, which meant his stride was more of a mince, though I wasn't going to mention that either.

He carried a box under his arm. From the way his biceps—revealed by the torn off arms of a very dirty T-shirt—bulged, the thing was heavy. Why hadn't he left it in the car?

"I've been callin' ye for nigh onto a minute," he snapped.

"I . . . uh . . . sorry."

"Come along. I don't have all day to be dallyin'."

He headed for the crowd he'd just popped out of. When he reached them and elbowed through without a word of pardon, I hung back, unwilling to follow in the wake of his rudeness.

"Keep up or be left behind," he shouted.

I kept up, though I murmured excuses and apologies all the way.

A Fiat, that was nearly as tiny as he was, idled at the curb. That would not be allowed in America. No unattended vehicles at airports. Did they have that rule here? No other car idled at the curb, but the security officer stood several doors down and didn't appear to care. In truth, he didn't appear to see us, which was strange, but lately, what wasn't?

I stepped toward the passenger door, only to be shouldered aside as my companion went there himself. When he opened the door, I saw why. The steering wheel was on that side of the car.

"Right," I muttered. "You drive on the wrong side of the road."

I wouldn't have thought it possible, but the fellow's scowl deepened. "Leave it to an American to decide which side is the right side."

He had a point. I scooted around the rear of the car and got in. The man struggled to set the heavy box behind us. I reached out a hand, and he jerked it away, before rising onto his knees and placing the heavily taped container on the back seat. He was starting to get on my nerves.

"I was just trying to help."

"'Tis my responsibility." He faced front and quickly merged into traffic.

"Seems heavy to be dragging around."

He lifted one shoulder. "It's too precious to be out of my sight."

"What—?" I began, and he interrupted.

"I'm Ben."

"Short for Benjamin?"

"No. Just Ben."

"No last name?"

"Screwed."

I blinked. "Your name is Ben Screwed?"

"With a 'K.'" He made an annoyed sound at my continued confusion. "S-k-r-e-w-d. Skrewd." He gave the word a bit of an Irish lilt. I still had to cough to keep from laughing.

"Just Ben it is," I managed. "Have you known Quinn long?"

"All of my life."

An odd statement. Ben appeared old enough to be Quinn's grandfather. He'd probably meant to say "all of *his* life." Considering his perpetual scowl, I decided not to correct him. I might be slow, but I could be taught.

Silence settled over us, broken only by the chug of the engine. I felt compelled to fill that silence. Maybe I couldn't be taught after all.

"Do you know what Fiat stands for?"

Ben slid his dark, button eyes in my direction before returning them to the road.

"Fix it again tomorrow," I said brightly.

Nothing.

"My . . . uh . . . husband had one when we first met."

Max had hated that car—a lemon from the day he'd bought it.

"I can fix anything with an engine," Ben said.

Which would explain the grease on his shirt.

We'd left the city and headed into the rolling countryside, which was a lot less green than I'd imagined. Weren't the hills of Ireland supposed to be so green they made your eyeballs hurt?

"How far to Quinn's place?" I asked.

"He told ye it was his place?"

"Isn't it?"

The old man shrugged. "Not more than forty kilometers or so."

A partial answer. I wasn't surprised. Ben seemed to dole out words as if they were precious gold. I had a sudden image of him in a leprechaun suit with a pot of the stuff. I coughed to cover my inappropriate giggle. It would only get me into trouble.

As would my admission that I had no idea how far forty kilometers might be. To say so would mark me again as a typical American, with little to no knowledge of or interest in the metric system.

The road became less of a straight highway, more a winding trail, the farther away from Dublin we went. In the distance, the sea swelled with whitecaps.

I enjoyed the scenery and kept my mouth shut until we crested a hill and headed into the village that filled the dale. The cloud cover was so low the place appeared shrouded in mist.

"Like Brigadoon," I murmured.

"That's Scotland."

"Glocca Morra?"

"There ye go. Though that was imaginary too."

I was surprised a cranky old coot like Ben knew anything about the musicals of the 40s and 50s. Though he'd no doubt been around then. I just liked them.

I was about to ask the name of the not-Brigadoon-nor-Glocca Morra village, when a sign flashed past naming it *Doras Dearg*. As every sign I'd seen thus far was printed in both English and Gaelic, I was able to read the translation: *Red Door*.

"Weird name," I said an instant before we reached the town proper, where every door was red. "Or not."

Ben continued through the village in the direction of the white-capped sea. The road curved so much, and the hills and the dales were so numerous, that it appeared for an instant as if we'd drive right off the edge of the earth and into that sea. Then a cottage seemed to rise out of the earth, and the road ended at its own bright red door.

"Was the town named after the doors, or were the doors painted red after the naming of the town?"

Ben cast me a quick glance. "A better question might be be; Why are the doors red?"

"Why?"

He sighed and got out of the car as if I'd asked him a hundred annoying questions, instead of only the one he'd proposed. "Red doors are found all over Ireland."

Ben snatched my bag and headed for that door. I scrambled up the cobblestone walk in his wake. "Why?"

If he was going to treat me like a three year old, I might as well act like one.

"To ward off evil spirits."

I laughed. Ben did not.

"Why?" I said again.

He opened the red door—wasn't locked, did the color red also keep out thieves?—then cast me a sour glance over his shoulder. "Blood of the lamb."

"I . . . what?"

"Have ye read yer Bible lately?" He didn't wait for my answer. "Blood of the lamb on the doorposts protected the Hebrews from the plague of the firstborn."

I knew that. What I didn't know was what it had to do with this.

"This is an ancient land," Ben continued. "With ancient legends and beliefs."

"Like the Hebrews," I agreed, and his sour gaze turned shrewd.

"Yer smarter than ye appear."

"Thanks?"

The sour returned.

"It's a symbolic connection then?" I continued, unable to keep my curiosity to myself. "Red paint instead of blood, evil spirits instead of the hand of God?" I'd heard of looser connections.

"Whatever ye say." Ben stepped inside.

The stone cottage had two rooms—one a combination living and kitchen area, the second a bedroom. That there was no third meant the bath . . . wasn't. Hell. How old was this place?

Handmade, glossy wood furniture gave the place a rustic air that was complimented by the rough-hewn cabinets and floor. The ceiling had appeared thatch from the outside, but inside it presented solid sturdy beams and tight planking that would keep the rain and wind out.

"No one really believes a red door turns away evil spirits, do they?"

"If not, then why have one?"

"You believe there are evil spirits?"

Ben's gaze met mine. "Don't you?"

I did. I'd seen them, but I was one of the few. And the one I'd seen . . . well, I doubted she'd be deterred by a red door.

Ben made a sound deep in his throat—both amusement and disgust—how did he do that? "The Irish are a superstitious lot. And the red doors are a bit pretty, aren't they?"

I nodded, my gaze on his face. Something in his dark eyes bothered me. "Why was the town named Red Door?"

That smacked more of a need for protection than a bit of pretty superstition.

Ben hesitated, then lifted one shoulder as if saying: *She'll find out anyway.*

"There's a local legend." He glanced out the back window, at a garden as overgrown as my own.

"Of evil spirits?"

"*Cat dubh,*" he murmured, sounding as if he were in a trance.

"Black cat?" I didn't know much Gaelic, but I did know the word for *black*. "A black kitty cat caused the entire town to paint

32

their doors red, then name the place that for good measure when they could have just—" I paused not wanting to voice what they could have done. "The Irish can't be that super-stitious."

Ben spun, fingers clenched. "'Twas not a pussy cat but a long, lean killing machine."

I resisted the urge to laugh again. He wasn't kidding.

I spread my hands to indicate the size of a tom cat, lifted my eyebrows. Ben shook his head and opened his arms wide, then emitted a snarl so vicious, the hair on my neck fluttered.

"That sounds like a—" I searched my mind for the right animal. Big, black, vicious cat equaled—

"Panther," Ben said.

A sudden image of the statue in my garden flickered. That couldn't be a coincidence, but what did it mean? And how should I ask? No idea, so I headed in a different direction.

"Are black panthers native to Ireland?" I thought not. They seemed more of a jungle creature.

Ben tossed my bag onto the kitchen table. "Of course not."

"Then how—"

"How does any creature walk the earth where it doesn't belong? They are abandoned, bereft." He sounded as abandoned and bereft as those he described.

"Why would an abandoned animal be the cause of a hundred and one red doors?"

"The *cat dubh* stalked these hills in a time when there were no phones, no television. The beastie would have been beyond our ken and therefore a cause for legend and superstition."

"What was the legend?"

"I don't follow."

"The red doors were used to keep out evil spirits. The black panther wasn't a spirit but form, an animal abandoned and bereft but not evil."

Ben spread his hands. Was he being dim on purpose?

"What did the big bad kitty cat do to gain him evil spirit status?"

"He did what all evil spirits do. He killed people." Ben left, slamming the door behind him.

He seemed awful mad about something that happened long ago. A time without phones or televisions? Had Ben even been alive? Who knew when they'd gotten electricity out here, though I thought it had to have been since Ben appeared. Perhaps one of his ancestors had been slaughtered. Still . . .

I opened the door. "That's what wild animals do."

Ben stood next to the Fiat. He didn't appear to hear me. The wind whipped off the sea at nearly gale force. I hurried after him, not sure why. What difference did it make if a long dead panther had been maligned for behaving like any panther would?

I reached the car. He continued to stare.

"Ben?" I followed his gaze.

The box he'd set on the back seat appeared as if it had been torn apart from the inside.

By claws.

# CHAPTER 5

"*W*here is it?" I asked.

Ben spun, nearly knocking me over. His gaze flicked around the yard, eyes so wide I looked around too. Nothing was there but grass and flowers.

"Where is what?" he managed, voice a bit hoarse.

"Exactly."

His scowl returned. "Ye aren't makin' sense."

"Whatever was in the box escaped."

He opened the car door. For an instant I thought he was leaving and experienced a moment of panic. Though the size of the box indicated that whatever had been inside wasn't large enough to cause true concern, the shredded remnants of said box did just that.

Having just flown, I had no weapon beyond what might be inside the house. I wasn't fast enough to outrun much, or strong enough to snap more than a twig. Considering what was trolling the earth these days, I wasn't certain anything I might find or do would help.

"Hey." I reached for Ben's shoulder. "Don't—"

He straightened, drawing from the floor in the back seat what appeared to be an ancient farm implement—wooden handle, curved stone blade. Add a black hoodie and he'd look like the Grim Reaper.

"Take it." He jabbed the thing at me. I moved out of swiping distance. The tool appeared both elderly and sharp. Getting cut with that was Ebola waiting to happen.

"What was in there?" I repeated.

"I am sworn."

"Good for you. What was in there?"

"I cannae—"

I lowered my voice, though we were alone. Then again, maybe we weren't. "I know about the Nephilim."

"I dinnae—"

"You do," I said. Though why he would bring one here in a box, I had no idea. He was a friend of Quinn's, not Liz Phoenix. Wasn't he?

"Did Liz send you?"

He ducked his head in a half bow. "No." He jerked his head up. "Who?"

"Nice try," I murmured. He knew who she was, but I didn't think she'd sent him. Did it matter?

I took the tool. If he knew about the Nephilim, and I kind of thought he did, the keeping of it in his car meant it would work on whatever the hell had been in that box.

"Is this a scythe?"

"Sickle."

"Difference?"

"Sickles were spoken of in the Old Testament. Scythes came later."

As we were dealing with demons that had been around since just after the fall, it was a sickle.

"What does this . . ." I pointed at the stone and lifted my eyebrows.

"Flint," he answered.

"What does flint kill?"

"Curved flint sharpened by a priest of the church, with a handle of wood from a place where the Israelites walked."

"Sheesh," I muttered. The thing was probably worth a gazillion dollars. And I was going to us it against . . .

I didn't have a clue.

"What is it?" I asked for the umpteenth time.

"It will not hurt you."

I lifted the sickle. "Then why this?"

He looked away. I wanted to shout *liar*, but right now Ben Skrewd was the only friend I had.

"Why would you bring a box full of Nephilim here?"

"'Twasn't," he snapped.

"Breed?" He frowned. Confusion? I didn't think so. "Grigori?" His frown deepened, and he didn't answer.

Was there another type of killing machine that Liz hadn't told me about yet? No doubt.

Distant thunder rumbled, and I glanced toward the sea. The mist had thickened, causing the sun to dim. But not a single storm cloud bubbled in the sky.

Ben's gaze flicked to the cottage and I spun, just as the shriek of a wildcat filled the air. My fingertips went numb and I dropped the sickle. The sharp end stuck in the ground with a muffled *thunk*. I barely missed my own foot.

"Stay here." Ben snatched the weapon then headed for the cottage. Instead of going in the still open red front door, he skirted around and made a beeline for the back.

"The creature probably can't cross the threshold," I murmured to myself, hoping the sound of my voice would calm my racing heart and still my shaking hands. It didn't. I kept talking anyway. "Red door keeps out the evil, black, spirit kitty cat, so it must be in the back yard and not the living room."

My laugh rang out, slightly hysterical. "Shh," I said, and

hugged myself. My hands were so cold, their contact with my arms only made me shiver.

I'd known about the Nephilim even before Liz had told me the score. I'd read the Bible. I'd studied the Testaments. More importantly, I'd read the books that had been left out. I was curious. *The Book of Enoch* had been a revelation.

Ha-ha.

I'd only seen one evil half demon in person. That had been enough. I never wanted to see another one again.

"Can't always get what we want," I said. Mick and Keith were definitely smarter than they looked. Who wasn't?

I waited as instructed, but after the initial growl, followed by the snarl-shriek, silence reined. Had Ben killed the creature? Had it killed Ben? Either way, there should have been more noise than the wind.

I crept across the yard, poised to flee, though the idea of fleeing from a demon panther almost made me run before I saw one. However, I couldn't leave Ben alone. I might have just met him; I didn't even like him. Nevertheless . . . it just wasn't right.

"Ben?"

Was it good or bad that he didn't answer? Nothing else did either.

I pulled out my cell phone. No service. No shit. I hadn't had the time, or the brainpower, to figure out an international calling plan. I shouldn't have even brought the thing.

My gaze roamed the area, hoping for a nearby cottage. Not a single thatched roof, not a chimney, not even a wisp of distant smoke appeared.

"Fan-damn-tastic," I muttered, one of Liz's favorite words. I saw the appeal.

I continued along the side of the cottage, skirting the woodpile, where I grabbed the biggest piece I could carry and took it along. I didn't like to confront demons empty handed. I took a breath, tightened my grip and stepped into the garden.

Nothing was there but flowers, veggies, me, and the sickle lying abandoned on the ground.

I picked it up. No blood. I looked around the yard. No cat.

And no Ben.

\* \* \*

IT WASN'T until dusk loomed that I considered driving to Red Door—I couldn't remember, or even pronounce the Gaelic version—or even to Dublin, in the car Ben had left behind when he'd . . .

Fled? Flown? Disappeared? Died?

I'd taken a quick tour of the garden, found not a trace of him —dead or alive. I had unearthed a panther statue, nestled in the neatly weeded corner of potato plants. The thing looked exactly like the one I'd left at home, right down to the eerie yellow-green eyes.

I'd thought the one in Milwaukee had come with house. But now, with plenty of time to think, I realized I hadn't noticed it until after Quinn arrived. Apparently he'd brought one along. The question was why? I'd think it was a statue of protection if the local legend hadn't been of a creature that everyone needed protecting *from*.

I stared out the cottage window as night fell over Ireland. Though there'd been no more snarls, I still wasn't keen on leaving the dubious protection afforded by the closed and bolted red doors—the back door was red as well—to seek out a Guinness and ask a few questions. Not to mention that I'd never driven on the "wrong" side of the road. I could probably manage that, but I never had learned how to drive a stick shift.

If there hadn't been more hills than people, I might have tried. But I'd observed enough folks who'd killed their engines on inclines. It was damn hard to get the thing started again and not roll all the way back down. The idea of being out there in the dark, alone in a flooded Fiat, made me draw the curtains and stay inside.

I kept a tight grip on the sickle. I'd probably sleep with it.

"Better than sleeping alone." I was really going to have to stop talking to myself.

"Tomorrow." When the sun was up and I hoped Quinn was here.

I wish I'd asked him when the next flight was. You'd think that was something he would have told me. Unless he'd been lying just to get me out of Dodge and had no plans to come here at all. Though that didn't sound like Quinn. Then again, what did?

Outside, in the dark, something went bump, thump, clunk.

"*That* sounded like him."

Thunder rumbled. Or maybe not thunder at all.

I stood in the center of the cottage with an ancient sickle clenched in my fingers so tightly I feared I'd never be able to unclench them.

More thunder snarled, unless it was a snarl that thundered. Then lightning flashed and I relaxed. A storm was the least of my worries.

The door rattled, and I dropped the sickle. Lucky I wasn't a demon fighter.

I leaned over and retrieved the weapon. I'd be no damn good at it at all.

The door rattled harder. "The wind," I said, as if saying it would make it so. Combined with thunder and lightning and the torrential rain beating on the roof, what else could it be?

The doorknob flicked—right, left, right. "Huh." Wind couldn't do that.

I opened my mouth to shout, "*Who goes there?*" then snapped it shut again. I hadn't turned on the lights yet. Better to pretend no one was home.

The front door stopped rattling; the knob stopped turning. I had just taken my first breath in what felt like several days, when the back door shuddered. Once, twice, again, as if something very big or very strong had slammed against it. I drew back the sickle in my best imitation of Hank Aaron, and the door burst open.

I expected a panther, what I got was a man. As the sickle would work on him too, I swung.

He ducked. The sickle hit the wall. Sparks flew. The impact caused my fingers to go numb and I let go of the handle. The man snatched the weapon from the air before it fell even an inch.

He straightened from his crouch. In the half-light the movement was leonine. Or perhaps it was just my overtaxed, panther legend-steeped brain.

"What the hell, Megan?"

I blinked. "Quinn?"

"I'm glad to hear the surprise in your voice." He lowered the sickle. "I'd hate to think you knew it was me."

I opened my mouth and a sound very like a sob came out. Quinn stilled. "Meggie?"

The next thing I knew I was in his arms, clinging, shaking, almost crying. I lifted my face. Our noses brushed. He felt so warm and strong, so familiar, so damn right that I kissed him.

Damn right.

\* \* \*

QUINN HAD BEEN SO startled at Megan's sob, he nearly fell on his ass when she threw herself into his arms.

He should have. He'd forgotten of late to be clumsy. Besides, if he'd fallen, she wouldn't have kissed him.

Unless he'd kissed her.

With Megan in his arms, so soft and warm and round, he couldn't think. With her mouth on his, he couldn't breathe. Then her tongue brushed his teeth, and he couldn't stop.

He tossed aside the sickle; she didn't seem to notice. Her

fingers had clenched in his wet shirt. Her nails scraped his waist and his pelvis arched toward hers.

She gasped when his hardness bumped into her. He clenched his own hands in her hair so that he wouldn't clutch her hips and grind her against him. He didn't want to scare her any more than she already was.

Guilt washed over him, colder than the rain. He'd wanted to arrive before now, but he hadn't realized how a return to this place after so long away would affect him.

She shivered beneath his hands. He pressed his mouth to her neck and gooseflesh rose, tickling his lips. He licked the pebbled skin. Her breath caught, and her breasts slid across his chest. Something else was pebbled too.

"Cold," she muttered.

Hell, he'd left the door open. He kicked it shut; the thing swung back open. He'd broken it. Fool.

The darkness within the cottage had terrified him. He'd called her name, but it had been torn away by the wind. The next thing he knew the door was open. And she'd swung a sickle at his head.

He snatched a chair with one hand, shoved it beneath the knob, considered lighting the fire and decided there was no time. He'd desired her from the first moment he'd seen her, loved her not long after that.

He wouldn't. He couldn't. He shouldn't. To touch her was death. He had been warned. Then she whispered, "Quinn?" in a voice full of both fear and wonder, and he was more lost than he'd ever been in his long, lonely life.

He swept her into his arms and carried her to the bed, yanked back the counterpane and laid her on top.

He could see her in the dark, all tousled curls and curves. Though she'd never said so out loud, he knew that she believed herself too round, matronly, even stout. He thought she was voluptuous and strong, and being a mother, giving birth, only increased both.

If it was death to touch her he would pay that price. He had waited eons for this.

He dropped his wet clothes atop his soaked shoes and stepped toward the bed as lightning flashed.

She held up a hand. "Wait."

He nearly groaned. If he waited, he would think, and if he thought, he would stop.

He *should* think; he *should* stop. This was insanity brought on by the storm and the night, her fear and his lust. Was there anything in that combination that didn't shout *mistake*?

"You're the most beautiful man I've ever seen," she whispered. "Can I—" She sat up, biting her lip, then reached out, her fingers pausing an inch from his stomach. Her gaze lifted, so much uncertainty.

Definitely a mistake.

He leaned forward, and her nails brushed his ribcage. They both stopped breathing. He stilled, waiting for her to remember who he was, who she was, where they were and why. Instead she pressed her mouth where her fingers had been and neither one of them remembered anything but each other.

She scraped her teeth along his hip, swirled her tongue around his naval. His cock brushed the underside of her chin and her head turned fast, like a snake, her tongue darting out like one too, laving his tip.

He jerked back. Such had never occurred to him. All he knew of desire had been born in her. He understood what was required—he was a man and a beast—but beyond that lay a mystery.

Her brow creased; she lifted her gaze. He'd done something wrong. He wasn't sure what.

Slowly she leaned forward and licked him again, then took all of him in her mouth. Shock made him stiffen; the movement pushed him farther within. The back of her throat rubbed against his tip, and the groan he'd been repressing broke free.

"Mmm," she agreed, stroking his buttocks, pulling him in and out of her mouth in a simulation of the act he craved.

He meant to stroke her hair; instead he buried his fingers in the riotous curls and held on.

Something built in his belly, spread outward like a slow flickering flame. He tingled everywhere. Did he glow?

Quinn opened his eyes. There was a glow, but it came from the flickering lightning beyond the windows and not from him. If he hadn't been half mad with lust he might have laughed at the idea of his skin sparkling, like the vampires in those foolish books and even sillier movies. Vampires did not glow, unless they were standing beneath the moon covered in someone's blood.

The image sent a cold dose of reality over him, and he stepped away again, shook his head to clear it and glanced at the barred door. As a lock would not keep out a Nephilim, the chair was laughable. However, the red doors would, which was why he had them.

Megan reached for him. He caught her hands. If she touched him again—anywhere—this would be over. He should probably let her touch so that this *would* be over before he did something more foolish than falling in love with her. Was there anything more foolish than that?

She was still completely clothed while he was naked as the day he'd been made. He would like to do something about that. He would like to do many things but . . .

Quinn glanced at the door.

"Oh, no, you don't," Megan muttered, and pulled off her shirt. Before he could stay her she lifted her hand, made a twisting motion at the center of her bra, and her round, soft, glorious breasts sprang free.

His mouth went dry; he couldn't move. Could only stand there like a fool and stare as she shimmied out of her jeans, revealing a slim silver chain about one ankle. He licked his lips, considered licking his way from that chain to her—

The lightning flickered, and she glimmered, her skin the shade of pearls. His dry mouth suddenly watered. His tingling hands began to itch. His cock leaped.

She was both life and death, everything he wanted, all that he craved. When she held out one hand, captivated he took it, and then he took her.

Soft and warm, so tight he gasped. Her fingers clenched on his biceps, nails digging in. Had he hurt her?

"*A rún mo chroí,*" he began.

"Shh," she whispered, eyes closed, face intent.

He wanted to stare forever at that face, remain for always just like this, never leave, never speak, never know anything else. Then she tightened around him, and he nearly disgraced himself, was only able to retain control by going still as a statue and counting in Gaelic.

*A haon, a dó, a trí, a ceathair—*

She ran her nails across his back and murmured, "Now, Quinn," and he forgot the word for *five*.

Was it the *now*, the *Quinn*, or the puff of that whisper past his ear that took away everything but need. He couldn't help it he thrust—just once, he promised, only that.

And then he was thrusting, pumping, coming. She was grasping, gasping, coming too. He thought the world shook with the force of their joining, but it was only thunder.

He had read books, watched movies, heard . . . things. He had imagined; he had dreamed. But he had not known; he had not understood. Because he had never touched a woman.

Until now.

# CHAPTER 6

When I awoke I felt delicious, and for an instant I just savored that without knowing why. I could not remember the last time my first thought on awakening had not been a worry—Max, the children, the bar, money, time, exhaustion, Liz.

"Hell." Thinking of what I wasn't worrying about made me worry. And remember.

I'd slept with Quinn.

While it had seemed like a good idea at the time, in retrospect . . .

I stretched, my body sore in all the right places. Images of the man, of me, of us, flickered like last night's lighting.

In retrospect, it had been a damn fine idea. One I wanted to have again.

I opened my eyes. I could see the entire cottage, there wasn't that much of it. Not a trace of Quinn, not even a stray sock. If it hadn't been for the soreness of my body, which hadn't been touched in so long I was surprised I wasn't half crippled, I might think I'd imagined him.

Was he in the bathroom? I frowned. There wasn't a bathroom.

Crap. I really needed a bathroom.

I clambered out of the bed, wrapped myself in a sheet and went to the window. The storm had blown away, leaving behind bright sunlight and a much greener Ireland than yesterday.

It had also blown away Ben's car.

However, I had more pressing issues right now. My bladder. As I wasn't going to traipse outside in a sheet, I found my clothes, and dragged the chair away from the back door.

Though the brilliant sheen of day made my fears of last night seem foolish, nevertheless, I picked up the discarded sickle and took it along. Despite popular literature, demons came out in the day as well as the night.

Upon further examination, the stone and plank building I'd thought a garden shed was not. I used it for what it had been meant then took a stroll through the garden. The rain had beaten down some of the plants, but the warm air and sun were perking them up. Still, something bothered me about the place. Something I couldn't put a finger on.

A car door slammed and thoughts of the garden fled as I followed the sound.

Quinn climbed out of Ben's car holding a takeout cup of coffee and a bag that smelled sweet and yeasty. The man knew what I needed.

His eyes met mine and everything that had happened last night rose up between us. I expected to be embarrassed. I'd banged my bartender. Instead, I only wanted to do him again.

"Morning," he said.

I just smiled, afraid that if I spoke my voice would break or wobble.

He held out the cup. "Double shot, nonfat latte."

"Here?" My excitement was so great my voice both wobbled and broke. I took the cup and downed a scalding gulp.

"You'd be surprised at what we have here."

My fingers tightened around the sickle. I didn't plan to be surprised again.

Quinn reached into the car and came out with another cup. His would be tea. Perhaps I knew him better than I thought.

"Ben," I blurted, and Quinn's eyebrows lifted as he sipped. "He disappeared."

Confusion filled his eyes, which appeared to have taken on the emerald shade of the grass this morning. The brilliant jeweled hue dazzled me. "I just saw him in town."

"But he . . ." I glanced toward the garden, and suddenly I knew what had bothered me about it. The damn panther statue was missing. Or maybe the thing had gotten buried in the potatoes.

I didn't realize I'd strode off until Quinn tried to catch up, caught his toe, spilled tea on his shirt and dropped the bag of yeasty goodness, which split open to reveal scones bursting with raisins. My mouth watered.

Nevertheless, I left him behind to gather them while I continued to the garden and used the sickle to push aside first the potato plants, then everything else.

No statue.

"What're you doing?"

"There was a panther statue here last night. Exactly like the statue in my garden in Milwaukee."

"Okay."

I returned to the place I'd seen the stone and used the sickle to stir up the ground. Had the rain fallen so hard it had gotten buried?

"Gone," I said. "Just like the one at home."

"I don't remember any statue, love."

"Here?"

"Or there."

"You didn't bring it?"

"Why would I do that?"

"I thought . . ." My voice trailed off. The statue wasn't the problem. Or at least it wasn't the biggest problem right now.

"There was some—" I paused. I'd been about to say some*thing*. But I changed it to— "There was someone here last night."

"Is that why you're carrying around the weapon?"

I followed his gaze, saw that I was still swooshing the sickle through the garden with the hand that wasn't around my coffee, clutching the thing as if it were a lifeline. "Yeah."

"And why you nearly took off my head with it."

"Sorry. I was spooked."

"You've had a rough few days."

I'd had a rough few years, but who was counting?

Me. However . . . I eyed Quinn. Maybe I could stop, or at least stop while we were here. A man who looked like him, who was basically a drifter, had to be accustomed with short-term affairs. I wanted one.

"The fellow who came to Murphy's is dead. He can't hurt you anymore."

He hadn't been a man, but we'd let that go.

"Ben told me about the *cat dubh*."

Quinn blinked. That *had* sounded mighty random.

"Then we heard a shriek. The box in the car was torn open. Whatever was in it was gone. Ben took the sickle into the back-yard and then . . . poof."

Quinn stared at me for a minute. "Maybe you should eat something."

"You don't believe me?"

"Ben didn't go poof. He returned to town."

"On the wings of angels?"

Quinn jerked and dropped the bag of scones again. If they weren't in crumbles by now, they never would be. "I don't understand."

"He left his car. How did he get to town?"

"That's my car. He was to leave it for you. He must have gotten a ride from a friend. Like I did."

"What about the box?"

"There was no box in the car this morn."

Didn't mean there hadn't been one, though I was starting to wonder.

"The shriek of the cat?"

"Cat's shriek, usually when they're . . . uh." He blushed. The man was an infuriating, enticing blend of sin and innocence.

"It wasn't that kind of shriek."

"And you know this how?"

"I've heard cats shriek when they're . . . uh. This wasn't that. And it wasn't a house cat." He opened his mouth, and I kept talking. "It wasn't a tomcat either. It was a big cat. A wild cat."

"The wind whistles off the sea sounding like many things. Hence the legend of the *cat dubh*."

"Ben said the thing killed a lot of people. The wind doesn't kill."

That I knew of.

Quinn's cup hit the ground and tea exploded, soaking into the already damp earth. He stared at it for a moment, then lifted his gaze to mine. "The *cat dubh* was a story used to frighten children into staying close to home."

"Yet the town is named Red Door."

"So?"

"Red doors keep out evil spirits." I lifted my chin to indicate the cottage. "You have two yourself."

"A charming tradition you'll see all over Ireland, as well as the UK. You truly think a painted door would bar evil from a threshold?"

Once upon a time, no. Today?

God, I hoped so.

* * *

"LET'S sit at the table to eat the scones." Quinn started for the cottage.

"I thought they were *scones*," Megan said, using the British pronunciation of the word, which rhymed with *con*, like *skawn*.

He set the bag on the table and rolled his eyes. "Please."

If there was one thing the Irish avoided, it was anything British.

She laughed. "I don't suppose there's any clotted cream." Her laughter faded. "No refrigerator."

He shrugged. No need.

"You have lights but no appliances. Not even a toilet."

"There's a toilet."

She gave him a withering glare. "That is *not* a toilet."

He experienced a moment of shame at the primitive nature of the place. However, its lack of amenities was one of the reasons it was so safe. The generator that powered the lights was fueled by propane, which anyone could buy. The water came from the well by means of an old-fashioned hand pump. He supposed he could put in a toilet and a shower, connect them somehow to the well and the generator, but that would involve workers and permits, payments and the like.

Would explaining all that arouse her suspicions higher than they already were? What kind of man kept a home that was off the grid unless he had something to hide?

A man who wasn't truly a man. One who might never be.

The thought distracted him so that when she moved to set the sickle on one chair at the same time he reached for the bag of scones-that-rhymed-with-cones, his hand connected with the flint.

He drew in a breath, dropped the bag, spun as the pain ripped through him, cradling his hand against his belly, waiting for things to get much, much worse.

But they didn't.

Megan leaped to her feet so fast her chair tumbled over. "Did I cut you?"

She yanked at his shoulder. He remained right where he was. He could not let her see.

"A little," he lied. "It's fine." He started for the door.

"Wait. Let me—"

"Eat," he said shortly. "I'll wash it at the pump. 'Tis nothing."

Quinn hurried to the garden. He spared a quick glance at the cottage. Megan stood in the doorway. From there she couldn't see anything important, so he stuck one hand beneath the spout and used the other to pump. Cool water gushed. He let it cascade over the appendage until she returned to the table. Then he stopped and peered at the mark caused by the brush of the flint against his flesh.

"*D'anam don diabhal,*" he muttered.

There was no way he could explain why his hand had been burned and not cut.

# CHAPTER 7

The scones were soft, light, fluffy, not burned at all. So why had I smelled that unmistakably acrid scent when Quinn had dropped them on the table?

I sniffed at what was left of my coffee but it didn't smell burned either. Perhaps someone had set fire to garbage nearby, and I'd merely caught a whiff.

Or I was losing my mind. Wouldn't be the first time.

Max's death had sent me to the edge. Only the kids, and Liz, had pulled me back. But I'd been close enough to feel that madness, sometimes I felt it still.

The scones were better than any I'd ever had in the States. Not that I'd tried any after the first, which had been dry, hard and downright nasty.

I had a sudden urge to try everything I'd ever heard was better here than there. Clotted cream, Guinness, wine, brown bread.

Irishmen.

I glanced through the window. Quinn was gone.

I ran to the front door, threw it open, let out a breath. He stood at the trunk of the Fiat, poking around within.

"You need help?"

He straightened and banged his head on the top, reaching up to rub it with his uninjured hand. "I'm good."

He had been. My lips curved. Maybe I'd try the clotted cream *on* the Irishman. Couldn't hurt.

"I've got a first aid kit in here somewhere. I'll be right in."

He continued to poke around in the trunk. I lost interest and returned to the table where I contemplated the last scone. I should really save it for him.

I waited as long as I could, which wasn't very long at all, and ate it. If everything here tasted like that, I was going to need two seats on the airplane when I returned home. Where my children were, or would be, should be.

My easy mood disappeared. How was I going to call them? What if there was an emergency and they tried to call me?

Quinn walked in, hand shrouded in gauze.

"Should you get that looked at?" I asked.

He shook his head. "It was in an odd place. I've cut myself before there. If I don't keep it wrapped, it'll just open again and again."

"I'd like to go to town."

"I'm fine."

He strolled to the table. I couldn't help but admire the view and agree. He *was* fine.

He lifted his eyebrows when he found nothing but an empty bag and coffee cup.

"We can get more in Red Door."

"I'm not going back to Red Door."

"I want to call the children. What if they have to call me? My cell has no service."

"I already called your in-laws, told them where you were, how to contact us if they needed to."

"You . . . Wait . . . What?"

"It's not aeronautics, Megan."

I blinked, then made the connection. "You mean it's not rocket science?"

"Aye," he agreed.

Sometimes he spoke like a little old British man.

"I brought you here to relax and get some rest. You won't do either one if you're worrying about the children."

"I always worry about the children." Even when they were sitting right next to me. I probably always would.

"You called my in-laws." I remembered Susan's question about Quinn and closed my eyes. "What did they say?"

"The children are having the time of their lives."

That didn't sound like Susan. She was not a "time of your life" gramma.

"They did seem a bit taken aback that you'd gone off to Ireland."

I opened my eyes. "You think?"

His face creased. "I don't understand."

"One of the reasons my in-laws take the kids is so that they can have a few weeks away from a mother who works all the time."

He still appeared confused.

"I never go on vacation. I have a business to run."

"Not any—" The light dawned. "I told them what happened." He lifted his good hand. "I asked them not to tell the children about the accident."

It had *not* been an accident, but I didn't want Quinn to know that. Would he move on down the line to the next job if he knew I was marked by demons? A day ago I'd have paid him and said, "Goodbye and good luck." Today I wasn't sure what to do, what to say.

"I gave your mother-in-law my number. I explained that the cell service was bad way out here, but that my phone worked better than yours."

"You told my in-laws that I'd left the country, and I'm staying in a remote cottage that has iffy cell service with my boy toy bartender. That's swell."

"I don't understand why you say it like that."

I spread my hands wide, waiting for him to catch up.

His eyes widened. "They think that I . . .? That you . . .? That we . . .?"

I snorted. "They thought that *before* you, me, we did."

"Why?"

I looked him up and down. "It isn't aeronautics."

He blushed. I'd never seen him do that at home. Then again, at home he'd been Quinn, the bartender, and I was his boss. Now . . . well, hell. The last of my good mood fled. Now, things might get awkward.

"What's a boy toy?"

Definitely awkward. "It means you and I, that we . . . " I waved toward the bedroom.

"Are lovers?"

This wasn't about love. Couldn't be. I needed to set some ground rules. Fast.

"Boy toy means we're having fun."

His eyebrows lowered.

"Just sex," I continued.

"Just?" he repeated. "There's nothing *just* about sex."

He had a point. I should try to explain better, though why I had no idea. He was a hot, young bartender. He had to have had a hundred one-night-stands. Double damn.

"We didn't use anything." He blinked. I *had* switched gears, but I was still on the same subject. "No protection, Quinn."

My voice was sharp. He winced, and I softened it. This wasn't his fault. *I'd* kissed *him*. What was he supposed to do? Run? He was a young man, and I wasn't that old of a hag.

"I'm on the pill." I had to be. The first few days of my periods were so heavy that without it I could barely drag myself from the house; there was no way I could work. "I won't get pregnant."

I'd once dreamed of having half a dozen kids. Silly in this day and age, but I loved kids, loved being a mom. I still did, though having to be a dad, as well, sucked.

"You sound sad, *a chéadsearc*."

My gaze met his. *He* looked sad. Most guys his age would panic at the very mention of pregnancy.

"I feel foolish. We should have used something, but I'm not . . . I haven't. Since Max."

"I know," he murmured. "If you're worried about disease ye needn't be. I would never be the cause of any harm."

"You're clean?"

"I am."

"You haven't slept with anyone since your last blood test?" I clarified.

His forehead creased. "I've never slept with anyone attall."

I laughed. "Right. You don't sleep. Ha."

"Megan, I don't—"

I lifted a hand. "Enough said." I did *not* want to hear details about his lack of sleep with other women. Oddly, it bothered me to think that there'd *been* other women. Which was stupid. As I'd told him before, this was sex, not love.

"Did my mother-in-law say anything else?"

His gaze went distant. "There was something about a cougar. I told her that the legend was about the *cat dubh*—a panther. She didn't seem to understand what I meant. Although I have no idea how she knew we were in *Doras Dearg*. I didn't tell her."

"Cougar," I repeated, and the light dawned. "She wasn't talking about the legend. She was talking about me."

*Bitch.* I wasn't that old.

"What does a cougar have to do with you?"

"Do you watch any television, Quinn?"

"Why would I?"

I suddenly realized I knew nothing about him after he left

57

Murphy's. Where did he live? What did he do? Who were his friends?

"What do you do in your free time?"

He looked away, lifted one shoulder. "Sleep."

"You work and you sleep?" Sounded like me.

His gaze flicked to mine. "You're changing the subject."

Was I? I hadn't meant to.

"Why did your mother-in-law use the word cougar?"

Maybe I had meant to.

"A cougar is a name for an older woman who likes younger men."

"You aren't older than me."

I laughed. He didn't. "Quinn, I'm at least five years older than you, maybe more."

"You aren't."

"How old *are* you?"

"How old are *you*?"

I resisted the urge to say, *I asked you first*, the childishness of which would only prove his point.

"Twenty-nine," I said. Though there were days, as well as nights, that I could swear I was aging in dog years—seven for every one—which would make me two hundred and three. That felt about right.

"I am much older than that."

"Prove it."

He opened his mouth, shut it again, tilted his head. "How?"

"Driver's license?" I held out my hand.

"I didn't bring it."

"Passport?" He glanced out the door. "You had to have that or they wouldn't have let you on the plane."

"I left it in the car of the friend who brought me here."

"Convenient."

"Not really." His gaze returned to mine. "Does age matter?"

"No." Age didn't matter. Lying did. Though I wasn't sure what, exactly, Quinn was lying about, I did know he was lying.

I was the mother of three. I could smell a lie as clearly as a recently soiled diaper.

* * *

QUINN'S HAND burned as sharply as his chest. He should probably breathe—not that lack of breathing would kill him—but he couldn't let out the air he'd taken in until she stopped staring at him as if he'd lied right to her face.

He had, but how did she know that?

The same way she knew when Anna had watched a show on the TV box that she shouldn't, or Aaron read a comic book instead of a schoolbook, or Benji ate everyone's candy.

"About last night," she began, and the breath he'd held in rushed out.

That she'd kissed him had been a miracle; that she'd touched him even more. The joining of their bodies had been beyond anything he'd ever dreamed. Who would dream something like that?

"We can't do it again."

He thought they could. In fact, he thought they could again right now.

"Don't look at me like that," she said.

"Like what?"

"Like . . . like . . . " She threw up her hands. "Like you're that damn *cat dubh* and I'm a mouse."

He froze. "Why would you say somethin' like that?"

She let out *her* breath. "You work for me, Quinn. It's taking unfair advantage if I—"

"I don't mind."

"I mind. My mother-in-law is a bitter, sad woman, but she isn't the only one who'd think badly of me for—"

"Who cares what anyone thinks?"

"I have a business to run. A small business in a local neighborhood."

"I don't understand."

"It might be the twenty-first century, but it isn't really."

He spread his hands. She wasn't making any sense.

"We might be living in a more enlightened age, but it still wouldn't be good for business if it gets out that I'm banging the help."

"We'll be quiet." At her obvious confusion, he continued. "We won't bang about at all."

One short, sharp laugh escaped before she quelled it. "I have small children."

"They aren't that small," he muttered.

"Quinn."

He sighed. "I'd marry ye—"

"Whoa!" She held up a hand. "I don't even know you."

He let his gaze travel from the tip of her curly red head to the toe of her well-worn shoe—not that long of a trip, but an enjoyable one—then lifted his eyebrows.

"That's not what I meant. We can't continue this . . ." She waved a hand toward the still rumpled bed visible through the open door into the bedroom.

"I understand. Back there you have children, the business, your friends and . . . his."

"Back there," she echoed, and her gaze went to the bed, stayed there a while. She licked her lips, and he wanted to do the same, even before they curved and her blue eyes met his. "In Milwaukee this ends. But here . . . "

"Here?" he repeated, both hoping she was saying what he thought and fearing it.

"Here I don't have anything else to do." Her smile broke free. "But you."

She took the few steps that separated them, bumping her

breasts against his chest. His hands clenched. The burn throbbed. He throbbed.

"All right?"

He knew what she was asking. He also knew what he must say. He might be able to explain away a single night in her bed as an accident, bad judgment, a mistake. But a dozen? Even half that?

Liz Phoenix would kill him.

He opened his mouth to refuse but the words that came out were, "All right."

# CHAPTER 8

*I* couldn't believe I'd suggested what I had. Sex for the sake of sex, no strings, the relationship would end when we returned to Milwaukee.

I wasn't fool enough to believe that we could "bang" away for two weeks, then pretend we never had. Either he'd quit when we returned, or soon after. If he didn't, we'd be in for awkward exchanges. We might get past that eventually, then again we might not. And what if he found another woman—he would, just look at him—would I be able to be happy for him and move on? I hadn't been able to move on from Max. Then again,

Quinn Fitzpatrick wasn't the love of my life, and walking away wasn't the same as dying.

Suddenly Quinn was right there, so close his breath brushed my hair. "You're thinking too much."

I looked up, and he kissed me. I forgot what I'd been thinking, saying, feeling. I forgot everything but this, but him.

Poor, pathetic, sex starved, older woman.

"Shh," I murmured into his mouth.

"Didn't say anything, love."

"Shh," I repeated and reached for his hand.

He winced and I realized I'd taken the hand I'd cut. "Sorry."

I lifted it to my mouth. Kissed the part that wasn't wrapped, tickled the base of one finger with my tongue. Next thing I knew he'd snatched my free hand with his and dragged me where I'd wanted to go in the first place.

His bed.

I pulled off his shirt, pressed an open mouthed kiss to his chest. He tasted so good I tried a nipple, the jut of his collarbone, then his hip.

The top button of his jeans gaped open. Convenient. I ran my tongue beneath the waistband, caught the tip of his—

He cursed and lifted me away with a fingertip to my chin. "I'll be no good to you if you keep that up."

"You'll be fine if you keep that up." I wiggled my eyebrows. He laughed, then seem surprised by it. "What's wrong?"

"Love is a serious business."

My happy feeling died. Love *was* a serious business. But this wasn't love. Couldn't be. I would never love a man again. Losing another would kill me.

"Quinn, I—"

"Shh," he mocked. "I know." He lifted his gaze, staring out the window in the direction of the garden. "'Tis all right."

His happy had died too, in more ways than one. I put myself to work restoring both, cupping my palm to his fading erection and lifting, kneading, squeezing just a bit.

Happy returned.

"You're always wearing too many clothes." He began to remove them.

I was tempted to dive beneath the covers before he could see the stretch marks on my ass, the pouch of three births below my navel. He didn't give me a chance. He put his lips to every mark, cupped my stomach with one large hand, and when I shifted away, set both hands on my hips and pressed his mouth to the soft, cushy skin.

He kissed and nibbled and laved until I was writhing. Who knew the belly was an erogenous zone? No woman with a belly like mine. Then his breath cascaded over my mound, stirring the curls, making me arch, and his tongue flicked just once.

My legs gave way and he caught me, lifted me, laid me on the bed. It wasn't until later that I wondered how I'd missed knocking him unconscious with a knee. How he'd managed to move so fast and with such grace. Considering.

He slipped into me with equal speed and grace. I teetered on the edge, tightening around him.

"Not just yet, *a thaisce*," he murmured, and stilled.

My fingers clenched, my nails biting into his back. His breath hissed in. "Sorry." I released him, and he set his forehead to mine.

"Ach, no. Just . . . do it again."

I drew my nails down his sides to his buttocks, scraped them along the skin and gooseflesh rippled. He began to move—first slowly, then when I continued the onslaught of my hands—nails, fingertips, nails again—faster. He gasped; I begged; we cried out as one.

When the tremors had fled and we lay side-by-side, I threw an arm over his stomach—not round or pouched but flat and rippling. I considered tracing the muscles with my mouth but the idea of lifting my head from his shoulder was too much.

"What does *a thaisce* mean?"

He'd used several Gaelic words since we'd come here but right now the latest one was all I could recall.

"Treasure," he murmured, voice slurred by sleep.

Treasure. I liked it.

I considered asking about the others, but from the way his body had relaxed against mine, and his breathing had evened out, he was gone to dreamland, or close enough.

I thought that was the second best idea he'd had all week and followed.

* * *

Quinn stood in the main room of the cottage. The room was dark, as was the night beyond the windows.

He smelled the sea, caught the distant glimmer of the moon. The door must have blown open—he never should have broken it —because the wind blew through the room, stirring his hair, making him edgy.

Something was coming.

No. Something was here.

The darkness became light in the shape of a woman, and he understood.

"Mistress," Quinn murmured, and knelt.

"I told you not to do that." Liz Phoenix planted her booted feet inches from his own.

Quinn straightened. "Why are you here?"

The leader of the light was taller than he remembered. Or maybe it was just because he felt smaller. He'd betrayed her trust, ignored her orders. He'd laid his filthy paws on her very best friend. Quinn doubted a woman who had been charged with thwarting the Apocalypse was going to be swayed by the excuse, "I couldn't help it."

Her blue eyes swept the cottage. "Is Megan all right?"

When she turned her head, her short dark hair, which she'd allowed to grow from very short to just plain short, not for vanity but to cover her new tattoo, shifted.

A phoenix took flight from the top of her spine. If she touched it, she would become one. Then she'd no doubt burn him to ashes. That wouldn't kill him but it would hurt like hell. More importantly, his rising from the ashes, just like the being that had caused them, would reveal to Megan Murphy the truth.

Quinn Fitzpatrick wasn't human. No matter how much he might long to be.

Liz's gaze flicked back, narrowed. "Quinn." She snapped her fingers in front of his face. "Got no time. Megan?"

"She's safe."

"I didn't come all this way when I'm in demons up to my ass so that I could leave without seeing for myself."

Why had she? The last he'd spoken to her shit had happened, and she'd had no time for him or Megan. Which meant it was very deep shit indeed.

Her gaze lit on the bedroom door, closed, and as it was the only door in the place, it didn't take a neurosurgeon to figure out where Megan was.

She strode in that direction, and Quinn bit his lip to keep from telling her not to. One did not tell the leader of the light not to do anything. Unless one wanted to become ashes.

Quinn didn't. Not yet.

Besides, he wore all his clothes. Just because Megan didn't would prove nothing. If he was lucky, Liz would see her friend was breathing and leave. He'd worry about explaining himself later.

Liz opened the door, and everything stilled. Quinn's hair stirred again, but this time it tingled, as did every hair on his body. The very air seemed sucked from his lungs, the room, the earth. A snarl rippled around the room.

Quinn rushed forward. There was no reason for Liz to be so furious unless—

His gaze landed on the bed and he blinked. He was both there —all tangled up in her—and here. How could that be?

"You are a dead man," Liz said.

"I know. Just don't kill me until she's safe." He met her eyes, which blazed like blue neon in the night. "No one will protect her like I can."

"That's protecting?" She nodded at the bed where he and Megan slept on.

"No one is closer to her than I at this moment."

"Max," Megan murmured.

He stilled as agony flared.

He could be at her side from now until forever, he could make love to her until she slept in his arms over and over again. But she would always love another.

Liz looked quickly away, but not before pity flashed in her eyes. He deserved it.

Quinn beckoned, and Liz followed him through the living room and out the still broken back door and into the moon-shrouded garden.

"I'm dreaming, aren't I?"

"What do you think?"

"You're a dream walker."

"I'm everything," she muttered.

Quinn didn't know much about his mistress. He'd heard she was a sexual empath; she absorbed the supernatural abilities of others through sex. Not the easiest way to save the world, one Quinn didn't envy, which was probably why he was a minion and not the boss.

Liz Phoenix had become leader of the light upon the murder of the previous leader, her adopted mother Ruthie Kane. She'd been thrown into the fight against evil, against doomsday, without time to prepare. Bad things had happened, but she was still fighting. Eventually she would win.

She had to.

While he hadn't known she had the power to dream walk—the ability to stroll through the dreams of the one with the answer to her most desperate question—he did know what it took to do so. One had to hover between life and death.

"Where are you?" he asked. "What happened?"

She waved away her mortal wound or terminal illness as if swatting a gnat. "I'm too far away for you to help, and what happened doesn't matter."

"Liz," he began.

"At last. It only took my imminent demise to get you to call me by my name."

"How imminent?"

"Damn imminent, or I wouldn't be in your head."

"What do you need from me?"

Her lips curved. "I didn't know I needed anything."

"Yet here you are."

When a dream walker walked, they did so in the dreams of the one who could answer their most desperate question. Which meant she was here for him. But why?

"Megan." Her head turned toward the cottage. "I was worried."

"Your most desperate question was for her welfare?"

She shrugged. "Go figure. But really, Quinn, if I'm not saving the world for her, who am I saving it for?"

"Everyone?"

"Everyone isn't real." She clenched her hands. "I don't know everyone. Hell, I don't like anyone."

Humanity was a large, teaming mass of faces without names, strangers who were mostly assholes. There was a reason the demons had been able to blend in for so long. A lot of humans behaved just as badly, even with a soul. So sometimes it was best to focus on the saving of the ones who mattered the most personally. He had.

"Does she know?" Liz murmured. "What you are?"

He shook his head.

"She knows what I am. All of it. She still loves me."

"I—" he began, then words failed. There'd been a time when he'd done terrible things. The time was long past, yet it haunted him. "Being friends with the leader of the light is far different than sleeping with . . . me."

"I'd hope so," Liz muttered. "Otherwise you aren't doing it right."

He wanted to smile at her jest, one she'd made before, but he couldn't.

"She's going to find out. Better that she knows before she sees." Her gaze went to the cottage. "Believe me."

Her eyes, her voice, her face were so sad. She'd been lied to. Who hadn't? But Quinn thought the lies that had been told to Liz Phoenix were earth shattering. Literally.

"I could be human before she need ever find out."

"Could be," she agreed.

She sounded no more convinced than he was. Probably because she still planned to kill him.

"I have to go. There's bad things happening. They might spill onto you, onto her, onto all of us."

"Don't they always?"

"Yeah. Keep her safe. Keep her here. I'll let you know when you can come back."

"The children are only with their grandparents for two weeks."

"It'll be over before then."

"What will?"

She smiled sadly. "Everything."

He wanted to ask more but suddenly the wind returned and lifted her off her feet, then dragged her backward and away, though the same wind only ruffled the ends of his hair.

# CHAPTER 9

*I* awoke from a dream of Max. Considering I was naked in another man's bed, that should have bothered me more than it did. Except in this dream, my dead husband had been saying good-bye.

He'd seemed okay with it too. He'd been smiling and behind him had been this golden, sparkling, blinding ray of light.

*You had to move on so I could*, he said.

I'd called his name, tried to run after him, but I couldn't.

"I can't stop loving you, Max." Not when Anna had his eyes and Aaron his nose and Benji his hair.

*You don't have to. The more you love, the more you love.*

"I have no idea what that means."

*You will.*

He turned, walked into that light, and I woke up. I waited for the usual despair to wash over me at the realization that I'd only dreamed of Max, would only ever dream of him because he was gone. Instead, I felt . . .

Better than I had in a long, long time.

I sat up. I was not only naked but alone.

"Quinn?"

No answer. Unless you counted the rustles and thumps from the living room. What was he doing?

I climbed out of bed, considered dressing, decided I needed a shower and wrapped the sheet around me instead. It was already torn off the bed anyway. Considering last night's activities I wasn't surprised.

I walked into the next room. "What are you—?"

Ben Skrewd turned from his perusal of the back door. Since he held a hammer, I assumed he meant to fix it. From the looks of the thing, he wasn't having much luck.

His gaze swept over me; he colored and spun about again. I glanced down. I was covered, but considering the sun glaring in from the front window behind me and his reaction, I was revealing more than I wanted to. I stepped into the bedroom and snatched up my clothes.

"Where's Quinn?" I called, trying to put them on without dropping the sheet.

"I'm not his keeper." *Thud. Crash. Bang.*

"Have you seen him?"

*Crack.* What was he doing out there?

"How do you think I knew to come and fix the door?"

"He called you?"

"I don't have a phone."

And that didn't even seem odd anymore.

"Where is he?"

"Still in town I suppose. I'm not his—"

"Keeper," I finished. "Got it."

I joined him as he shut the door. It creaked open once again, and he cursed in a language I didn't know. Which meant it was anything but English.

"Problem?" I asked.

"I know how to fix a bloody door." He tossed his tools back into their container with more force than necessary.

They clattered and clanked, the sound making me wince

71

nearly as much as the idea of a *bloody door*.

"I'll have to order a new strike plate. This one's busted beyond repair."

"Okay. What did you do with the box?"

His fingers tightened around the handle of his toolbox and, for an instant, I thought he'd leave without another word.

"Quinn said it was gone," I continued. "So you must have taken it."

He turned back. "It was an old box, why wouldn't I?"

"It wasn't an old box when we got here. It was a box full of something with claws."

"If there was something alive in there, it wouldn't have been for long without air holes."

I tried to remember what the box had looked like the first time I'd seen it. Not that large but seemingly heavy. I couldn't remember if there'd been air holes or not.

"Why do you care about some old box?"

I didn't care about the box; I cared about what had been inside. It had to be some kind of Nephilim.

"You gave me the sickle to kill it."

"Kill what?"

"You tell me."

"I have no idea what yer gettin' at."

The weapon lay across the table. "Why did you give me that?"

"It was all I had, and you seemed nervous."

"You want it back?"

"Don't need an old farm tool any more than I need an old box."

He left. I was glad. I didn't want to give him the sickle. Whatever had clawed its way out of the box was still loose. Ben could deny all he wanted that there'd been anything inside, but I knew better.

Quinn had no idea what was out there, but I did. The idea of that beautiful, sweet, klutzy man fighting a creature of hell, dying because of it, because of me, terrified me nearly as much as the creatures themselves. So I'd protect him from death-by-half-demon with whatever I had, even if it was only an old farm implement and the iffy magic of a painted red door. It was the least I could do.

I propped that door closed again with the chair, otherwise it kept inching open. I caught the scent of fresh paint, sniffed, followed my nose and saw that Ben had painted a stripe of red across the threshold, from one door jam to the other.

"Superstitious old coot," I muttered. But what did my relief at seeing it make me?

The afternoon waned and night approached with no sign of Quinn, and I started to worry. What if his car had broken down on the way back? What if he was walking along the road and darkness fell and the *cat dubh* found him? Did it even have to be dark for the creature to appear? I had no idea. Regardless, Quinn was safer with me.

I picked up the sickle, topped with that beautiful, curvy sharp piece of flint.

The house was too small, too stuffy. I stepped into the back yard, taking my sickle along for company. The setting sun glinted off something in the overgrown garden. I only had to take a few steps closer to see what.

The damn panther statue was back.

I stared at it, captivated, and the yellow-green jeweled eyes blinked, just once.

"Impossible." I took a step back. But I knew better.

I'd once seen a woman disappear into a wisp of smoke. That had been the extent of my encounters with the Nephilim, but I'd heard stories from Liz. Nephilim were evil, and they wanted to kill us just for the pleasure of it.

The thing's tail twitched, beginning to unfurl from where it curved about the body. The muscles beneath the fur coat rippled.

For the first time I noticed that the shoulders looked a bit human, and—

Since when did a statue have a fur coat?

"Shit," I muttered, and tightened my fingers around the handle of the sickle.

I should have run, but I was frozen with both fear and fascination.

The statue was no longer stone but flesh and fur, lengthening, growing. It glistened, black as approaching night, sleek and beautiful and deadly.

Then it saw me and emitted that same wildcat call I'd heard last night. Every hair on my head, and everywhere else, tingled.

"Fuck me," I muttered, and turned. Only to find my path blocked by something worse.

My mouth fell open as the dragon spread its golden wings and blew smoke out its nostrils.

The panther plowed into my back, causing me to fall flat on my face. But at least the blast of flame missed me.

The grass wasn't so lucky. I could smell it burning, feel the heat near my feet. I lifted my head just as the panther landed on the dragon's back, its claws sinking in and causing the creature to snort fire again. I rolled, narrowly missing another burst of flame.

"There's a dragon," I said, as if saying it would make it more believable. It didn't. If the flames hadn't convinced me, talking to myself certainly wasn't going to.

The panther's shriek sounded like *Run!* Probably just my brain screaming the same word.

I was nearly to the door before I remembered the sickle. I spun, saw it on the blackened grass, considered going back for it. Then the dragon, blood flowing from the gashes the cat's claws had opened in its neck, swung in my direction. The panther still clung, even though the creature's wings beat furiously, smacking into the cat on its back over and over, sounding very much like an approaching helicopter.

The dragon's scales rippled like muscles. Its onyx eyes lit on me, and the dragon drew in a breath so deep all the air around me seemed to disappear.

I dove for the cottage, knowing I was dead, still needing to try. I landed on the floor, considered covering my head, realized how dumbass that was and flipped onto my back, hoping I could kick shut the open red door.

No time. The dragon released fire. I waited for the flames to roll in and over me. Instead, the dragon squealed like a little girl as the flames seemed to hit the red door, even though it wasn't there, then blow back the way they'd come.

The big scaly, serpent with wings got a face full of fire. The golden scales turned black and fell to the ground, one by one. My gaze dropped to the line of red paint across the threshold. Ben Skrewd hadn't been so superstitious after all.

The panther still clung to the dragon even though the creature's body was wreathed in flame. The dragon twisted and turned, writhing, roaring. I put my hands over my ears, but I could not tear my eyes away.

In its death throes, the dragon spouted fire again, only to have it bounce off the invisible door and into its face once more. The second dose accelerated the blackening of the scales, and within minutes all that was left of the beast was a pile of ash-covered squares.

The panther landed on top of that pile and the scales broke apart like fine china, becoming dust, blowing away on a sudden ill wind. The cat stopped screaming; the lump of fur and bone and flesh stopped moving.

I was still on the floor of the cottage, up on my elbows so I could see. I lay my spinning head down for just one second. What in hell had just happened?

The statue had come to life as a panther then fought a golden dragon. I needed to tell Liz. If I could find her.

Ash swirled above me, drifted down, and outside something moved.

I sat up so fast my stomach lurched. Or perhaps my stomach lurched because the panther that had so recently been a lump of dead, wasn't.

He rose, lithe and sleek, from the ashes. He stretched, shook and came toward me. I couldn't tear my eyes from his. There was something so familiar about them.

I should have been more afraid. A panther that doesn't die by fire is a very dangerous panther indeed. But he couldn't reach me. I was beyond the red door.

Closer and closer he came. He paused at the threshold, and then . . .

He stepped in.

I scrambled backward. He kept coming. My shoulders banged against the far stone wall. My heart thundered. I should have returned for the sickle. Except then I would have burned.

Which was worse? Death by dragon fire, or death by shape shifting panther?

A hysterical burble of laughter escaped, and the animal paused. His head tilted. His yellow-green eyes blinked once and suddenly, I knew him.

"Oh, no you're not," I muttered.

His head tilted in the other direction, and so many things made sense.

The statue that had appeared in my garden. The one so like it that had appeared here. The box that had been torn apart from the inside. The way my bartender had suddenly stopped tripping.

"You may as well do whatever voodoo you do," I said.

And in the next instant the beast became the man.

# CHAPTER 10

Quinn coughed. A puff of smoke came out of his lips and drifted upward. That was probably going to happen for a while.

Megan slowly got to her feet. "What the hell are you?"

She looked furious, and he couldn't blame her. This was quite a big secret to keep. He should have kept it. Would have if she hadn't looked so afraid, and then . . .

She'd recognized him, and he hadn't any other choice. He couldn't keep lying to her. Not now that he'd touched her. It wasn't right.

But then neither was he.

"Gargoyle," he said.

"Gargoyles are made of stone," she snapped, then glanced out the door. "Oh."

He shrugged, realized he was naked, didn't care. All he cared about was her.

"How could you come through the door?" she asked.

"It's my door."

"But the red paint protects against evil."

"I'm not evil," he said. At least not anymore.

"All right." Her shoulders, which had been stiff and tense, relaxed. "I suppose that must be true since the dragon fire didn't —" She stopped. "Why was there a dragon?"

"*Paiste,*" he said.

"Is that what it is or who it is or why it is?"

"*Paiste* is a fire-breathing serpent that's been here since the beginning of time." Quinn ran a hand over his face. His palm came away gray with ash. "St. Patrick tried to banish him after he'd expelled the serpents, but he died before he succeeded. St. Murrough gave it a go, but he was only able to confine the beast to *Lough Foyle.*"

At her frown he continued, "A part of the River Foyle in Ulster. Northern Ireland."

"Then what in hell was it doing here?"

"'Twas sent." Now Quinn frowned. "Released. Murrough chained the thing beneath the water. It thrashed about so that the water there has strange tides and currents."

"Not anymore," she muttered. "Won't someone notice?"

"Notice?" he repeated.

"That the tides are no longer strange and the currents have gone back to normal."

"As they haven't been normal since around the fifth century, I doubt anyone knows what normal is." He lifted a shoulder. "People see what they want, explain it as best they can. They certainly aren't going to conclude that the dragon beneath the waves has died."

"Good point. Why would someone release it?"

"A panther is the top of the food chain, love. To kill me, they'd need somethin' special."

"You're not a panther. Not really."

"When I'm a panther, I am a panther. Really."

"A panther couldn't burn and then rise from the ashes like a phoenix."

"I'm not a phoenix."

"You aren't going to deny that one sent you."

He didn't answer. He had no defense against the truth.

"Liz ordered you to watch over me even though I told her not to."

"Liz Phoenix does what she likes, and listens to no one on this earth."

Her scowl deepened. "She's lost too many soldiers in her anti-doomsday army. She shouldn't spare any to protect me."

"She'd do anything for you." *As would I.*

"What was this?" she murmured.

"A battle. I won."

"Won't more Nephilim come?"

"No doubt. But it'll take them a bit to find another dragon." Or something worse. They needed to be gone from here before that happened.

"I meant . . ." She hesitated, chewing on her lip before lifting her gaze to his. "What was *this?*" She waved her hand between them.

He had to bite his tongue to keep from saying: *Love.*

He'd only embarrass himself. She'd asked for two weeks, and he'd agreed. Just because he loved her, would always love her, didn't mean she could ever love him. Even before he'd revealed himself to be inhuman, she'd murmured her true love's name while still wrapped in Quinn's arms.

He turned away before he said or did something even more foolish than what he'd already said and done.

"We agreed to enjoy each other while we were here," he said.

"That was when I thought you were human."

If he'd needed any more proof that she regretted what had occurred he would have had it. "There are times when I am."

"I don't think you're ever truly human, Quinn."

He was glad he still faced away so she could not see his pain. All he'd ever wanted was to be human, even before he'd met Megan Murphy.

79

"You should probably explain exactly *what* you are."

"I told you—"

"Gargoyle. But what does that mean?"

He took a breath, let it out, then began. "Long ago when the angels fell, those who'd rebelled were tossed into the pit. Some that hadn't rebelled were still too corrupted by the earth to return to heaven."

"They became fairies."

"Aye. They had no idea how to survive. Suddenly human—"

"Fairies aren't human."

He let out a breath and faced her. "They are and then again not."

"Like you."

"It's complicated."

"What isn't?" Megan muttered. "Go on."

"The fairies would not have survived without help. They got it from the beasts. As a reward for their aid to what had once been creatures of heaven, who might still be again, those animals were given the gifts of flight, of shape-shifting. They could sprout wings and turn to stone."

"You can sprout wings?" He shook his head. "I guess no one can have everything."

He didn't want everything. Just one thing. Quinn shoved his wants from his head. The way Megan hovered near the door, as if she wanted to run from him made him ache. She would never want him again.

"Eventually the fairies could manage on their own," he continued. "The powers that be," he lifted his chin toward the ceiling, "tasked the gargoyles with protecting the weak and unwary innocents from demon attacks."

"I'm neither weak nor unwary."

"You are innocent."

She snorted, then her gaze sharpened. "What did the powers that be offer in return?"

He looked away again. "Why would you think they offered anything but the joy of helping others?"

"Spill it, Quinn. You've gone this far."

"Humanity," he said, then met her gaze. "The more humans we save, the more human we become."

"Why would you want to be human?"

He blinked. "Excuse me?"

"You can't die."

"I assure you I can. Why do you think Ben gave you that sickle?"

"To kill you?" Her voice was incredulous. "I thought he was your friend."

"Ben Skrewd is no one's friend. He's a gremlin."

Megan opened her mouth, closed it again. "A what?"

"Gremlin. He's a cranky old fellow who can fix anything with a motor."

"Sounds like a bad-tempered mechanic."

"He is. Except he uses magic when things get very difficult."

"Wait. I read about gremlins. They were invented between the World Wars to explain problems with the aircraft."

"I assure you that gremlins have been around much longer than that. They just weren't noticed as much until planes began to fall from the sky. And gremlins didn't cause the problems, they tried to remedy them. I'm sure they were around the airplane motors more than usual. A creature such as Ben would be fascinated by an engine that could allow someone to fly without wings."

"What did they work on before there were motors?" At his curious expression, she continued. "You said gremlins were around a long time. From what I know about your kind, you were here before there were engines."

"Wheels needed to be fixed as well, love."

She let out a short, sharp laugh and rubbed her eyes. "Is anyone just a person anymore?"

"You are." Which was why he longed to be. Foolish, really. She didn't love him, couldn't love him, wouldn't love him. So why become human for her?

He had no idea, all he knew was that he craved humanity with the desperation he'd once craved blood.

"Why would Ben think you'd hurt me?" Megan's gaze searched his and uncertainty flickered. He hated seeing it there but he couldn't blame her.

"Liz would never allow me near you if there were any chance I might."

Her uncertainty fled. "That's true, but then why the sickle?"

"There was a time, long ago before I'd saved many when I did hurt people. I killed people. I can't blame Ben for being uneasy. I'm the reason for all those red doors."

"You're the *cat dubh*." She had to have known this, but she hadn't yet said it out loud.

"Aye."

She nodded, considering. "You came here as a statue, in that box."

"I did."

"Why?"

"I must spend a few hours in every twenty-four as a panther—flesh and blood or stone—doesn't matter. There was no way I was going to get a panther out of one country and into another, and I don't have a passport, so . . ."

"You became the statue and sent yourself Federal Express."

"Close enough. Once here, I . . ." he paused, not wanting to admit what returning to Ireland after so many years away had done. But this was a time for truth, so he told it. "The smell of the air, the feel of the place called to what I'd been. I shifted and the box . . ."

She made the motion that mimed explosion. "Boom."

He shrugged. 'Twas as good an explanation as any.

"How did the Nephilim find us?"

"I've no idea." Betrayal, most likely, but by whom, how? And if it had happened once, it could happen again. He had to make certain it didn't.

"Where's Liz?"

"I've no idea about that either, though . . ." He paused and something in his face made hers pale.

"What happened?"

"She spoke to me in my dream last night."

"Dream walking?" He nodded and she cursed. "That means she's hurt or nearly dead." Her lip trembled. "By now she might be completely dead."

"She isn't."

"You're sure?"

"When the leader of the light dies, we know."

"How?"

"We just do. DKs and seers are secret." Or at least they had been until recently. "Only the leader of the light knows all of their identities. If he or she dies before passing the knowledge on, we feel it, and we're drawn to the new leader."

Silence settled over them, but only for an instant before she blurted, "The children," and swayed.

He stepped forward and she cringed.

"I'm sorry," she said. "It's just . . ."

"They're safe. There are others like me watching over them."

"Just like you?"

"Perhaps." He had no idea who, or even what, had been sent. "I have to get to them. Now."

"There is no getting there now, *a chroí*."

She cast him a sour glance, and he waited for her to ask the meaning of the word.

*My heart,* he thought. *Mo bheatha.*

My life.

She looked away. "Says the man who can turn to stone and grow a tail."

83

"I cannot fly," he said, wishing, and not for the first time, that he could.

"Are there any dragons on the side of light?"

"Not that I know of."

"Something, anything, that can fly us across the ocean?" He shook his head. "Teleport?" Quinn frowned, confused, and she made an annoyed sound. "Get us from here to there in a blink."

"Not even the leader of the light can do that."

She swayed again, and this time he knew better than to touch her. "If anything happens to them, Quinn, I'll never forgive you."

He didn't think she was ever going to forgive him anyway.

* * *

I PACED while Quinn used his cell phone. Odd that his worked, then again maybe not.

The man I'd slept with was a gargoyle.

I stifled the hysterical giggle. *There* was a sentence I'd never thought would run through my brain.

He'd saved my life; he'd no doubt do so again. However, if anything happened to my children I'd rather he not bother.

Quinn snapped the phone shut and turned to me. "They're on their way."

"They're . . . what?"

"I sent Ronan to—"

"Who the hell is Ronan?" I was shouting. I couldn't help it.

"He's a . . . well, he's two things really. I don't think there's a word for him yet."

"That's just great."

"Ye needn't worry. Ronan is very trustworthy."

I wasn't going to touch that. My head was already pounding.

"Do you think I'd send anyone who was not?" he asked quietly.

He was right; I knew that. It was just . . . they were my babies.

They always would be. The idea of them on a plane, flying across the ocean, alone, or even with Ronan, whatever he was—

"I want to go to them."

"No," Quinn said, and opened his phone again. I grabbed it and threw it across the room.

"How are you going to get them out of the country? Please tell me you aren't turning them into stone and shipping them in a box."

"We can't turn humans into us."

"You can just turn yourself into humans."

"Only God can do that."

"God will make you human," I repeated. Another sentence I'd never thought to hear. "My in-laws would never allow anyone but me to take my children."

"As far as your in-laws know, you did."

I gaped. "What did you do?"

"You've seen me turn into a man when I was a panther. You think there aren't beings that can turn into anything, or anyone, that they want? Why do you think I sent Ronan, besides his loyalty and huge muscles?"

"He's a shifter?"

"Among other things."

"And he turned into me?"

"Do you have a better idea?"

"Yeah, take me home."

"I can protect you better here."

"They already found us here."

"Which means they'll find us anywhere. There's a traitor, a leak, something. I know this land; I have friends here."

"You mean the villagers who are scared of you?" He lifted one shoulder. "You have an odd definition of friends."

"We stay," he said.

"How long?"

"Until Liz tells me it's safe to go."

"The kids are supposed to start school in less than two weeks."

"Oh, well," he said, and retrieved his phone.

"Oh, well?" I repeated. "You might not be aware that I just finished high school and became a mom and now I own a bar."

Confusion wrinkled his brow. "I'm aware of everything about you."

My cheeks heated. "I meant that I can't teach them."

"You can do anything you set your mind to, Meggie. You always have."

For an instant I lost myself in the admiration I saw in his eyes, then I shook my head. "They'll get behind, I—"

"We'll enroll them here. They'll learn Gaelic. It'll be an adventure." I opened my mouth, but he kept talking. "It's have them come here to be with you or have them stay there without. A bit of lost schooling is the least of our worries."

He was right. Again.

"Okay."

His eyebrows lifted. "I don't think I've ever heard you so agreeable."

"Nearly being incinerated by a dragon can have that effect."

The rest of the day passed quickly enough, considering there was no television or radio. I'd at least had the presence of mind to pack a book, but I couldn't concentrate.

Quinn had Ben bring us food. When the old gremlin arrived I could do nothing but stare at him, trying to discover something that would have marked him as different if I'd thought to look. Like Quinn, there was nothing.

Darkness fell. I began to get twitchy.

One bed in the house and last night we'd shared it. I'd enjoyed the interlude as much the second time as the first, but now that I knew the truth . . .

Quinn stood and I tensed so violently the book in my lap tumbled toward the floor. He snatched it before it could hit the ground.

"Good catch."

"I do my best."

"You aren't lame."

"No?"

"Why did you pretend to be?"

"I was trying to appear human."

Oddly, it had worked. Although, would I have marked him as inhuman if he moved with the same speed and grace he did now?

Maybe.

"Why did you sleep with me?"

"Why did you sleep with me?" he returned.

"I—" My fingers tightened on the book. "Wanted to."

His lips curved into a sad smile. "I needed to."

Need. Want. Two things I hadn't given in to for a very long time and only with one other man. But what about him?

"Do you have sex with a lot of human women?"

"None."

"Why?" Unease flickered. "Am I going to have kittens?" How in hell would I explain that?

"Of course not."

"Because something like you and someone like me can't?"

"No, because you take birth control."

"Oh." I rubbed my forehead. Obviously something like him and someone like me could, hence all the beings that both fought against Liz Phoenix and fought for her.

I probably shouldn't have spoken about what had happened between us as if it were something that might have gone on in a zoo. Certainly, I was freaked that I'd had sex with a gargoyle, but that didn't mean the sex hadn't been fantastic. Something I wanted to remember fondly.

But the more I considered what he was, all he could do, the more I thought that a little pill wasn't going to stop anything.

"You're certain?" I pressed.

"I've never done it before, but—"

"Just because you've never impregnated a human before doesn't mean—"

"I've never had sex before."

I laughed. He didn't. I stopped, and he looked away, cheeks darkening.

"Wait a second."

He'd said that before, and I hadn't believed him. The idea of a man like him, at his age, never sleeping with a woman was unbelievable. But now that I knew he was so much more than a man . .

.

"Look at me."

Slowly he turned his face toward mine, and in his eyes I saw the truth. "You're a virgin?"

"No longer."

"Why?"

"I never met anyone like you."

What was so special about me?

He glanced out the darkened window. "I have to go."

"What's out there?"

"Nothing will hurt you."

"I know." Nothing had hurt me while Quinn was on the job, and I knew, without a doubt, nothing would.

"I have to shift," he said. "It's time."

"What if you don't?"

"I can't stop it. If I wait too long I'll just—"

His eyes suddenly shimmered, going from human light green to panther gold.

"Can I watch?"

"You watched me change from panther to man."

I had, but I'd been a little distracted by the fire breathing dragon that had just died, so I hadn't observed as well as I should have.

"Now I'd like to see the reverse. Is that a problem?"

He glanced toward the glass again. I followed his gaze and

saw his reflection flicker. "I waited too long. It's happening. Put me outside when it's done. I need to guard y—"

He crumpled, there was no other word for it. One instant he was a tall, dark, handsome man, the next his very being folded inward. His skin went gray and shrunk. His eyes went panther; he sprouted a tail and ears, some fangs. I tried not to blink; I wanted to see it all. But eventually I had to, and when my lids lifted, Quinn was a statue once more.

I lifted him with shaking hands, strode to the back door then the garden. I'd just reached the tangled mass when the shriek of a big cat split the night. I whirled.

Out of the darkness stepped another black panther. I bobbled the gargoyle, and it fell toward the ground.

Right before it hit, the thing changed. Instead of stone bouncing then shattering, a second panther crouched.

"Quinn," I murmured, and let my fingers trace his back. Beneath the ebony coat, muscles bunched.

And then he was gone, bounding toward the intruder, snarling. The two bodies collided, rolled, massive paws shot out, spiked claws scraping, shredding. Blood flowed. I had no idea which panther was mine.

Mine. Huh. I'd examine that thought later. If we survived.

One of the creatures gained its feet, swung its head in my direction and snarled. The revelation of fangs gave me a sudden desire to run inside. Fantastic idea. I did so and retrieved my sickle.

When I returned, they were rolling and slashing and bleeding again. Only death would end it.

The moon peeked over the horizon, spreading silver across the grass, across them. Their ebony coats shone slick with blood, the ground was spotted with black dots of it.

One of the beasts managed to fasten its fangs on the other's throat. Instead of waiting for surrender, it jerked its powerful head, ripping out the other's jugular. Blood sprayed. The degree of viciousness made me think Nephilim, which meant the dead panther was Quinn.

"No," I whispered. Hot tears threatened to blind me.

The creature stalked in my direction. I tightened my grip on the sickle. I could lop off its head and hope for the best, but what if . . .

I stretched out the blade, brushing its tip along the panther's fur.

*Zzzt!*

The scent of burned hair and ozone rose along with a thin veil of smoke. That didn't mean this creature was Quinn. It might just mean they were both gargoyles.

Shit. Now what?

It stood between me and the cottage. No red door test unless it moved.

Then the panther's snout lifted. Tiny sparkles of light swirled around its head like a drunken bunch of fairies. *Was* it a drunken bunch of fairies?

*Quinn Fitzpatrick.*

The voice came from those lights, neither male or female, but something in between. I was too bowled over by talking lights to feel the level of gratitude I should that the panther was Quinn and not . . . whoever.

*You have gained humanity. Bow and accept the gift.*

The panther shimmered, shifted and became Quinn. My breath caught. He'd done it. He was going to become human and then . . .

Then I'd have to think twice about ditching him.

# CHAPTER 11

*T*he sight of Megan with the sickle, uncertainty on her
face, fear in her eyes, had made Quinn want to shift so
she could see it was him and not the other, but he hadn't been in
gargoyle form long enough to return to his human one.

However the lights—God, an angel, who knew?—had trickled
over him, through him, and then he became himself and he was
glad. Because only as a human could he voice the inevitable.

"I choose to remain what I am."

The lights, which had been swirling so madly they made his
eyes hurt, paused.

"Quinn?" Megan whispered.

He ignored her, gaze on those lights.

*You have killed legion. You have saved multitudes. It is your destiny.*

"No," he said. "She is. And if I'm human, I can't protect her
against those that aren't."

"Quinn, don't."

If he was a gargoyle, he would lose her. He'd seen that truth
the instant she'd seen what he was.

But if he accepted his due, that gift he'd worked so long for,
the humanity he'd strived even harder for once he'd found her—

then she would die. No one would protect Megan like he would. So he would protect her always.

He had no choice.

Besides, even if he were human, she would never love him. The only man she would ever love was Max. Quinn had hoped it might be different once he was different, but he knew better.

*Choose, Gargoyle. Humanity now, or never?*

"Never," he said.

*So be it.*

"No!" Megan ran forward, but it was too late. The stars swirled up and away, as Quinn turned to stone.

* * *

HOURS LATER, when he was able to walk on two legs once more, he found her at the kitchen table. At the first sight of him, she gasped.

He looked down. Clawed, bitten, bloody. He was a mess.

"Your hand," she said.

He turned it over. His hand was fine.

"The cut healed."

"'Twas a burn, but aye."

"What about those?" She waved at the marks on his body. "Should I clean them?"

The idea of her running a damp cloth all over him made him turn away so she would not see what those words did to him.

"They'll heal." If he'd been less human and more gargoyle they would have already.

"Quinn?" When he didn't answer, she stood and came closer. "Why did you give up what you wanted so badly for me?"

"You'll die, Megan. I can't allow that."

"There are others who could protect me."

He turned. "None would protect you like I can."

She searched his gaze, then she reached for his hand, tangled their fingers together and held on when he would have pulled away. "Why is that?"

"You heard the sparkly lights. I've killed legion."

"Oh." She looked down and sighed. He'd disappointed her somehow. "I thought maybe . . ."

"What?" He discovered himself running his thumb over the back of her hand and stopped. His nails were crusted with dirt and panther blood. Maybe dragon blood too, it was hard to tell. He tried to tug free again. Again, she tightened her hold.

"I thought . . ." She lifted her eyes, swallowed, then swallowed again. "I thought you might have done it because you loved me."

"I'm stone, Megan."

"Stones don't bleed."

"I'm a beast."

She shrugged. "Who isn't?"

"I will never be human."

"Because you chose to give that up for me. Why?"

He couldn't speak; he couldn't think. He wasn't sure what to say.

"Come on, Fitzpatrick. You faced a dragon and who knows what else. You can't be afraid to tell a woman you love her."

"You love Max," he blurted. "You said his name in your sleep."

Sadness flickered over her face. "I'm sorry if that hurt you. He came to say good-bye."

Quinn frowned. "Good-bye?"

"I'll always love him. But he's gone. He isn't coming back. You're here, and I don't think you'll ever leave."

His eyes met hers. "I won't."

"I swore I'd never love another man."

Quinn's throat went tight. She didn't love him; how could she? "I understand—"

"I don't think you do. Losing Max devastated me. I didn't think I'd survive it again, so I cut men, love, sex from my life." She

93

shrugged. "Didn't miss it." He scowled, and she laughed. "Until you."

"You're going to have to explain just what in hell you mean, Meggie."

"You're damn hard to kill, Quinn."

"Aye."

"That's just what I need. You're who I want."

"Because I'm hard to kill?"

He wasn't sure he liked that.

"I'm not saying this right. I don't love you *because* you're hard to kill. But it sure makes loving you easier."

Before he could get the sense of that through his head—she loved him?—Megan kissed him, and then he couldn't make any sense at all for quite a while.

Eventually she lifted her mouth from his. "Never leave?"

"Never."

"Don't die."

"I'll do my best." He felt compelled to clarify something. "You understand that I was given a choice. The one I made means I'll never be human."

She touched his face. "You're more human than anyone I know."

She believed it. How strange.

"It might be a bit difficult to explain why I never grow old, and you do."

"That sucks." Her hand fell to her side as she wrinkled her nose. "The way you and Liz tell it, we'll all be lucky to grow old at all. Explaining your lack of wrinkles and gray hair is going to be the least of our worries."

"I'll never let anything hurt you," he vowed.

"I know."

"Nor the children."

"The children!" She glanced at the window, through which the morning sun shone. "How long before they arrive?"

"A few hours yet."

"We should probably shower."

"We?"

Her lips curved, and his body responded as bodies do. She led him toward the still broken red door. "A few hours might be just enough time."

## The End

# BLUE MOON

Winner of the RITA® Award for Best Paranormal Romance!

**When darkness falls, another world comes alive ...**

The summer I discovered the world was not black-and-white but a host of annoying shades of gray was the summer a lot more changed than my vision.

Call me Jessie, or better yet Officer McQuade. On the night the truth began, our usually shy wolf population near my hometown of Miniwa, Wisconsin attacked. At the scene of the first crime, I found a wolf totem, which lead me to Professor Will Cadotte, an expert in Native American mythology, particularly of the Ojibwe.

From day one, he annoyed me. Tall, dark and gorgeous, he was also funny, smart and nearly as sarcastic as I am. I felt things when I looked at him. I wanted to keep feeling them longer than was healthy for a woman like me. I know what I am. Better off alone.

Nevertheless, we began to work together in an attempt to determine what was rotten in Miniwa. We were getting nowhere until the arrival of Edward Mandenauer, a self-proclaimed werewolf hunter.

Sure, I laughed. Then one of our dead bodies walked out of the morgue. After that . . . things got really strange.

Now a rare Blue Moon approaches, making me wonder: Who can I trust when the moon is full?

BLUE MOON

# DEAR READER

Dear Reader,

Dances With Demons is a departure for me within the world of The Phoenix Chronicles as the narrator is not Liz Phoenix but her best friend Megan. I always liked Megan. She's got brass. I hope you agree and that you enjoyed this small look into her life.

I am often asked where I get my ideas. In the case of The Phoenix Chronicles, after reading a tidbit about the Nephilim "somewhere" my imagination took off. The more research I did, the faster my thoughts tumbled, then out popped Liz Phoenix. From that point on, writing these books was as much of a roller coaster as reading them.

Reviews are critically important to authors, so if you enjoyed this book, please consider putting up a Review (it can be as short as you'd like) on the platform where you purchased it. I would appreciate it very much!

I love hearing from my readers and can be contacted via my website (LoriHandeland.com) through Facebook (Lori Handeland Books) and on Instagram (Lori Handeland Books).

Subscribe to my NEWSLETTER for all the latest updates. Learn about new books, sales, and the occasional freebie.

I look forward to seeing you there!
Lori Handeland

# ABOUT THE AUTHOR

Lori Handeland is a five-time nominee and two-time winner of the prestigious RITA™ Award from Romance Writers of America, as well as the New York Times and USA Today bestselling author of over sixty novels spanning the genres of paranormal romance, urban fantasy, contemporary romance, historical romance, historical fantasy and women's fiction. Her novel *Just Once* received a coveted, starred review from Library Journal and was optioned as a feature film by Catalyst Global Media.

Lori set her sight on being an author at the age of ten. She remembers sitting at a typewriter before she knew how to type, pecking out a story about a family who went into space. As an only child her summers were spent with that typewriter, television, and, above all, books. As a young adult, she got sidetracked by the need to make a living. She worked as a waitress and later enrolled in college to become a teacher.

Lori lives in Southern Wisconsin with her husband of over thirty-five years. In between writing and reading, she enjoys long walks with their rescue mutt, Arnold, and visits from her two grown sons, awesome daughter-in-law and perfectly adorable grandchildren.

# MORE BOOKS BY LORI?

I have written over sixty novels, novellas and short stories across multiple genres. But whether you read a contemporary or a historical, a women's fiction or a paranormal, you will always find my signature voice, along with a little humor, a little angst and the depth of characterization and fast-paced plot lines I love to read as well as write.

You can download a complete LIST of my novels on my website.